The Sinners of New Orleans

The Story of Isabella Amadour Smithers

The Sinners of New Orleans

By Candace Hill

Sumley Publishing

Visit Candace Hill's choice publishing company at www.SumleyPublishing.com
Published by Sumley Publishing, 223 Town Center Pkwy. #1472, Spring Hill, TN 37174

Cover photo by Sam Hill. Illustrations by Sam Hill.

Printed in the United States of America.

Acknowledgments

I wish to thank those past editors that gave me a chance to express myself in my newspaper columns and travel articles. I wish to thank all of my readers who understood my need to give it up and fulfill a life-long dream and create this book. I wish to thank the publishing company that took a chance on a first time fiction novelist. I wish to thank my husband, Sam, for capturing images that help tell the story. And to Paul and Joanne who believed in me and helped to edit those first drafts.

A huge hug and bow down to my daughter and to Lee Wilson who both understand the need to "perform."

Last, but certainly not least, I want to thank the people of New Orleans for they served as the inspiration that haunted me, thrilled me with their spontaneity and spirit to always "Let the Good Times Roll!"

-Candace Hill

Contents

Candace and Sam Hill

A Statement From The Author

I fell in love with the city of New Orleans in the 1980s and have traveled there too many times to count. It is a city where new comers either love it or hate it. Some think it's dirty, smelly and too many weird characters on the streets and don't feel safe there. I just sort of smile and shrug my shoulders because it's all of those things, but so much more. It keeps drawing me back. The smells are coming from the finest restaurants, the dirt is like any big city and kudos to the sanitation companies that clean up after tourists have let their hair down and partied. And as for the characters, they are the inspiration for this book.

Thirty years ago a large woman sitting on a stool at one of the lesser bars fascinated me. I noticed that patrons seem to know who she was, but they gave her a wide berth when passing her to take a booth or another stool. She sat quietly sipping her beer and speaking to no one. I was taken by her dress of a brightly colored caftan, her long salt and pepper hair and the gaudy jewelry she wore. She was there when we went in and remained there when we left. But her image and demeanor remained in my thoughts for all those 30 years. I found myself looking for her whenever we returned, but to no avail. I began making up stories about her in my head and thought that someday I will write a book about that woman.

This story is completely fiction. All names, characters and incidents are purely the imagination of the author. Any resemblance to events or persons, living or dead, is coincidental. It contains a potpourri of images inspired by the city and the people I observed. It is dedicated to them.

-Candace Hill

The Sinners of New Orleans
The Story of Isabella Amadour Smithers

PART ONE

Chapter ONE

Lyn

Lyn walked out of the blazing French Quarter sun and into *The Sinner's Cup.* The heat was immediately replaced by the coolness of inside and the darkness caused her to stop until her eyes adjusted to the dim light.

She approached the corner of the mahogany bar and reached out to steady herself.

"What can I get cha," the bartender Caleb asked? "Can I just have a drink of water, please," she answered.

Caleb had never seen this woman before, but in the Quarter strangers were always dropping in for a quick one, asking questions and departing never to be seen again.

He placed a glass of ice water in front of Lyn and turned his back to finish drying the Pilsners.

Lyn took a long drink, sat the glass down and continued to stand in the same spot. She looked about the bar as if seeking a familiar face. Caleb turned back around, "Something' else," he asked? A meek no was all that Lyn answered and then gathering her nerve she asked Caleb "is she here?"

Caleb knew exactly what she was asking, but only mumbled and tilted his head to the left pointing to the back booth. "Will she see me," asked Lyn. Caleb just shrugged his shoulders and turned back around.

Lyn continued to stand at the corner of the bar, took a big deep breath and then determined, but with small steps walked toward the back of the bar. Caleb watched out of the corner of his eye as this tiny wisp of a woman walked toward Isabella Amadour.

Isabella's reputation was known throughout New Orleans. Lyn had pictured Isabelle Amadour in her mind. They had met years ago, but the image in front of her did not conjure up what she remembered.

Back then Isabella had been a real beauty. Shapely and always dressed to the nines, she had an air about her that bordered on royalty and certainly demanded respect. This lady before her was old and haggard.

Isabella was huge. She was dressed in a caftan of many colors, with numerous bracelets, rings on every finger, dangling hoop earrings and her salt and pepper long hair hanging down passed her breasts. Lyn could not help but notice that Isabella took up the biggest part of the large round booth in the corner. As Lyn remained silently standing in front of Isabella staring at this woman of legend, Isabella sat very still, her eyes shut tight. A Cigaretto sat burning in the ashtray and a half- finished drink beside it.

Just as Lyn was about to clear her throat to get Isabella's attention, Isabella opened her eyes and stared at Lyn. A long silence prevailed, as they seemed to size each other up before Isabelle finally spoke, "do I know you?"

Lyn was shocked at the deepness of her voice probably brought on by years of smoking those little cigars.

"Miss Amadour, we met long ago. I've come to you for help," Lyn answered.

"What makes you think I can help you girlie? I don't know you and by the looks of you I don't want to. You are disturbing me. Can't you see I'm busy? Go away." The harshness of Isabella's retort only temporarily wavered Lyn. She stood her ground.

"I said go away. I don't do those bones and cards anymore, so I am of no use to you girlie. As for advice, see someone else. Get out and let me get back to my work." Isabella was now quite irritated.

"But Ms. Amadour, I am at my wits end and have no one that can help me. A friend of yours….

"What friend girlie? I have no friends," Isabelle interrupted. "I can't help you, no one can!"

Isabelle began to rise from her booth, but the weight of her body caused her to fall back into the booth.

"What do you mean, Ms. Amadour, that no one can? I know you see things. I really need your help. I have no relatives to turn to and my friends are all afraid to get involved. My husband walked out on us three months ago and I don't even know where he is. Please, please just listen and tell me what to do. I don't have much money, but I'll give you all that I can, if you will just help me." Lyn was pleading, but knew she was getting nowhere with Isabella Amadour.

"Creaky's here Isabella," shouted Caleb from the bar.

Walking through the door of the *Sinner's Cup* was Isabella's rumored nephew, Gerald. Known by all in the Quarter as Creepy, the nickname was changed to Creaky due to the old wooden wheelchair that he pushed Isabella Amadour to and from her apartment around the corner from the *Sinner's Cup* bar where they spent most of the day.

Creaky could see that Isabelle was holding court with a woman he thought he might recognize. She was dressed in jeans and a T-shirt, but even with her back to him as he approached the booth, he was sure he knew that red hair and ass. Isabella waved him toward her and then Lyn turned around.

"Escort this woman out of MY bar, Creaky. I want to go home now," Isabella demanded.

Creaky knew from the rasp of Isabella's voice and the unusual loudness that she meant business and proceeded to take Lyn's arm by the elbow to push her toward the entrance of the bar.

The fear and anxiety in Lyn's eyes did not help to soften Creaky's grasp. She was beginning to lose her confidence. In spite of Lyn's staggered steps and begging not to be dismissed, Creaky only looked forward and upon opening the door pushed Lyn out, shut the door and bolted it. He then returned to Isabella's booth.

"What was that all about," he inquired? "Do you know who that was?"

Isabella found a small sliver of the full ashtray in front of her, stubbed out her cigaretto, downed the last of the drink and began sliding to the edge of the booth in effort.

"Hell, I know who she is, and don't much care Creaky. Her fate is doomed. She's no concern of mine."

Creaky hollered to Caleb to come and give him a hand getting Isabella into the wheelchair. It took both men using much of their strength to hoist her into the chair.

"You need to buy a new chair, Isabella," said Caleb. "I'll take it out of your paycheck mister. Shut up," was all Isabella remarked.

Creaky pushed Isabella out the door while Caleb held it open. "If that girl comes back, Caleb, throw her out, you hear me? See you tomorrow. Sell booze and mind your own business….MY business you twerp."

"My, but you are in high spirits today," Caleb laughed.

Creaky and Isabella walked in silence except for the constant creak of the old wooden wheelchair. Walking northwest on Barracks Street and rounding the corner on N. Rampart Street, they headed for Isabella's apartment building. It was a real fix-up piece of property, but she was lucky to have a ground floor and three rooms. It was small, run down, but it was home.

"Run to the grocers and pick me up dinner. I'm in the mood for something other than that horrible po' boy you brought me for lunch. And stop and get me some Abita and a pint of Jack too. Here's a fifty. Don't keep the change Gerald, I know what it costs. Now help me get in and to the couch." Isabella was great at giving orders and tossed him the keys.

"One thing dear "Auntie", what do you know about that woman," Creaky asked?

"Why does she concern you, dear "nephew," she grinned the only smile of the week. She doesn't know or realize her fate. And I don't want to get involved. She is in over her head. Should have minded her own business and concentrated on them kids instead. Now there is hell to pay. I know." Isabelle had a distant look on her face and then she closed her eyes.

"I know stuff too ya know. Word is that that woman knows something she's not supposed to know. But how do you know? I mean other than what you know, how do you know? You must still have some power, right?" Creaky was searching Isabella's expression for some kind of answer.

Isabelle shot Creaky a look that meant to really shut up. "Go to the grocer."

As soon as Creaky was gone, Isabella gave a sigh of relief. She thought to herself she should have never let Creaky see Zomba or tell him of the eyes' visions. She wasn't even sure what had ever possessed her to share such a secret. It most likely would be her doom someday.

Giving up her power completely had been impossible. Isabelle could still zero in on those that had needs, but remained silent and uninvolved. It was safer. Those days were gone, but would never be forgotten.

As Isabella lay in bed wishing for a night's sleep not disturbed by the demons of the past and the ones she was sure to see again, Lyn was hailing a taxi cab to take her to the Lake Shore airport where a private plane awaited her. Carrying only a small bag and a purse full of one hundred dollar bills, fake ID and a small caliber handgun, she was relieved that her children were safe for the time being at a closest girlfriend's house. She would make arrangements for them to join her as soon as she was sure it was safe.

Strapping herself into the airplane seat, she leaned back and closed her eyes awaiting take off. As the plane lifted off, she began to relax somewhat at the thought of having escaped.

She couldn't help but smile at the Oscar-winning performance she had just pulled off in front of the *New Witch of New Orleans*. "That fat ass doesn't have a clue," she said out loud.

Lyn knew she could not leave her hometown without testing Isabella's powers. She felt reassured and confident if Isabella really was all people said she was, then Isabella would not have dismissed her.

Lyn's life had changed so drastically in the last five years. Being from a prominent New Orlean's family had its perks, but they were fading. Emptying her trust fund, and connecting with her Daddy's old cronies, she knew that she had used up any and all favors accorded her from her previous life. She was on her own now and had to be cautious and smart.

The mansion she had grown up in on Coliseum Street in the Garden District was now in disrepair. Her Daddy had taken his own life with the same hand gun she now carried in her purse following the scandal at the bank and now she did not know where her husband Kurt was. Frankly she did not care. She had her own power now and her freedom.

It had been a lovely wedding when Kurt and Lyn married in front of a small congregation at Felicity Methodist. In spite of her father's objections to marrying Kurt, he wanted the ceremony to take place quickly. Lyn was three months pregnant. So he agreed to all the trimmings, walked her down the aisle and then handed his only daughter over to a man he did not like. Mr. DuCote was forced to invite some of the prominent people in his life such as the Mayor and the bank president, but told the upper echelon of the city that this was a private affair for his shy daughter. He did however invite those people he could count on to help make his and his daughter's life a little more comfortable in light of financial problems looming. The reception at the Elms Mansion on St. Charles was amass with flowers, champagne and a grand dinner delivered from Antoine's where the DuCote name still owned the $10,000.00 per year private table.

All of that had disappeared like the lights of the city as Lyn flew away. Destination: Amite, Louisiana. Amite is small town just north west of the Ponchartrain, but miles away in terms of the life style of the Crescent City and far enough away in real miles to feel lost.

The pilot of the small Cessna turned to speak to Lyn and the sound of his voice startled Lyn from the regressed thoughts of the past. "Excuse me miss, we should be in Amite in about an hour. We are northwest of Maurepas and I have radioed my buddy in Amite to turn on his runway lights."

Chapter TWO

Isabella Amadour

A precocious child, born with a head of dark hair, olive complexion and wide dark eyes that haunted you from the time she drew her first breath, Marta was destined to regret having her. By the time Isabella was five years old, it was apparent to Marta that she had brought into the world a child that asked too many questions, possessed the ability to play whatever role she needed to play in order to get her way. She innately knew when to whimper, throw a temper tantrum or play a sensual flirty smile that resulted in mischievous fun.

For Marta it was a challenge to raise her. For Isabella it was a childhood of confusion trying to figure what role to play.

Marta admitted to herself only that it was in her genes. She too had been a wild child growing up in the stilted cabin near Chauvin where the waters were full of danger, but provided safety from the outside world. It had been a hard life living among the gypsies that had migrated a generation before to the Louisiana swamps from the foothills of Mt. Codrului near the border of Hungary. She only knew her grandmother as the old woman that laid dying in a bed that smelled of urine. The men all ignored the women while they fished, drank liquor and sat near the open fire pit speaking in mixed languages of French, Acadian and an Indian dialect that resulted from the Cajun people.

With little to no schooling, Marta had few friends outside of the small band of distrustful people that were her family. Days were spent mostly alone dreaming of a different life. The road that was now extending further into their reclusive lifestyle was calling to Marta. With a history of running away, sometimes for days at a time, Marta at fifteen decided to take that road, and began the long walk to the big city. Defiant and determined with little more than the clothes on her back, a knife and a loaf of bread baked that morning she started her journey and never looked back.

Isabella noted that her mother was in a good mood that night at the table and began asking the same question she still wanted answers to and never got.

"Mama, who is my father, please, please tell me," she asked with the most sorrowful face she could imagine she was making.

Marta got up from the table, turned her back and responded, "Not again,

Isabella.

What difference does it make who he is or where he is….he ain't here!"

"But Mama, I have a right to know, don't I," she whined?

"You don't have any rights child. Shut up and eat your stew." Isabella knew

then Marta's good mood had faded and her constant question was the cause. Marta

left the room to get dressed to go to her job at the Pearl on St. Charles where she

would spend the next six hours in the hot kitchen cooking.

"I don't know when I'll be home. Finish your homework and go to bed. Lock

the door after I leave. Don't you dare leave this house, do you hear me?" And in a

whiff of Evening in Paris perfume, Marta left Isabella to fend for herself once again.

Isabella picked up her books and settled herself at the table to finish her

assignments. She had been a good student and even enjoyed going to the Academy.

She didn't quite fit in with the other girls, however and kept to herself.

After completing her English assignment, she grew bored with philosophy,

pushed them all aside and retrieved the Tarot Cards from her mother's side table. She

chose the Page of Swords as her significator and began spreading a Major Arcana for

a simple read. Handling the cards in just her left hand, which is closest to the heart

and more truthful, she began turning the cards just as her mother had taught her.

All seemed to be going positively when she discovered that the questioner was

designated as the Queen of Swords which generally signified her mother. She never

seemed to turn a card that might represent her father, but then again she knew nothing about him and therefore could never be sure. "Oh, I get it, cards, you want to talk about Mama," she said aloud.

One by one she revealed the cards from side to side in a consequence spread using only the Major Arcana.

On card four she revealed the King of Swords upside down. This had to be a dark man from the past and its positioning in that manner meant the next card revealed would explain who it might be. Isabella slowly turned the next card and saw The Tower in the future position.

The Tower was her least favorite card that usually meant there was trouble ahead. And very soon. As she continued to turn the cards and trying to understand their meaning, she became very nervous and her hands began to shake. She realized her heart was pounding quickly and then she felt light-headed. Only three more cards to turn. She hesitated. But not to finish the reading is dangerous and so with a deep breath she turned the next three cards. The Moon card told her there was deception ahead and The Judgement card in reverse told her there was about to be loss and separations. The final card was the overall outcome and it turned out to be the reversed Chariot. Now this was truly confusing to Isabella. She interpreted that as trouble with a vehicle and they didn't even own a car!

A sudden shudder came over Isabella and she sensed someone in the room with her. She turned and looked about to find she was alone, the house was quiet, very quiet, but there was a chill running through her body as if it were in a draft. The lights in the room began to flicker. She went to the door and double- checked its lock. Then just as she was about to check out the rest the apartment, she felt warmth and a sense of deep relaxation. She was suddenly very tired and needed to lie down. What was happening to her? As she sat down in the old chair and laid her head back, she could not resist the weight of her body as it sank into the softness of the old cushion. She slipped into a deep, coma- like sleep.

Isabella was startled out of her deep sleep by the pounding on the apartment door. Confused and dazed by the sound of the pounding and voices outside, she shook her head, wiped her eyes and glanced at the clock on the table. It was 1:10 a.m. Now she could make out what the voices were saying, "open the door, it's the police."

Isabella ran to the bedroom and turned on the light to find that her mother was not in her bed. It hadn't been slept in and Marta was not in the apartment.

Isabella approached the door cautiously and asked, "Who is there?"

"Is this where Marta Amadour lives," came the reply?

"Yes, that's my Mama," she answered.

"Open the door miss, this is the police."

Isabella stared at the door. She reached up and undid the chain, opened it slowly and meekly peered out into the dark hallway. "My Mama is not home sir and I am not allowed to open the door," she said.

"Young lady, we need to talk to you in regard to your mother. There has been an accident. What is your name?"

"Isabella Amadour, sir. Is my mother with you? Is she ok?

Isabella undid the chain and opened the door to see two police officers, the man speaking to her and a woman officer standing slightly behind him.

They entered the small apartment and noted the dim lights, the shabby furniture and the girl now known as Isabella to them.

"Do you have any siblings, or anyone in the city you can stay with," the female officer asked?

The next twenty minutes were a blur in Isabella's mind. She could hear them speaking to her, asking so many questions, but never answering hers. Finally the female officer sat down beside Isabella and explained that her mother was run over by a hit and run driver on Canal Street. She had been killed instantly. The investigation of witnesses implied that it was an intentional hit and only after they found her purse were they able to identify who she was and where she lived. They needed Isabella to notify a relative and to escort them to the morgue for positive ID.

Isabella did not cry. Wise beyond her years, and with the capability of thinking quick on her feet, she told the police officers that she would contact her aunt to come to the apartment. Together they would make all of the arrangements necessary for her mother. That seemed to please the officers for the time being.

After identifying her mother at the morgue, a police cruiser dropped Isabella off in front of the apartment building and once she entered, the cruiser pulled away. Isabella climbed the stairs to her apartment, walked in and sat down in the old chair.

This is a nightmare she thought. What am I gonna do? She had very little money. She was still holding the packet she had been given by the police with details of what needed to be done in order to claim her mother's body. She had been informed that the body could only stay in the morgue for ten days. Arrangements had to be made. Isabella's mind was working feverishly. She had lied about having an aunt and somehow they had believed she was 18 years of age. Otherwise she would not have been allowed to view her mother's body or been allowed to return home.

Isabella knew there was an old strong box in the top of the closet that included important papers. Money was a priority. Perhaps there was insurance. She needed a funeral director. Forget school. No time for that, but she would need to inform them that she would not be returning. She would get a job. She looked in the mirror at herself to see did she really look of age?

It was only after she stopped thinking of herself, did she begin to question why anyone would deliberately want to harm her mother? She was unable to answer any of the police officers questions about what may have happened. "What was Mama doing on Canal Street?" She was supposed to be at work, she thought. The officer said it had happened around 10:00 p.m. Why had it taken so long for them to notify her?

All of a sudden, Isabella recalled the reading of the Tarot cards. The Judgement and Chariot cards had predicted her mother's fate. Could the cards now help her in what needed to be done next? Would the story be in the newspapers blowing her only chance to protect herself from outside forces? Could she just disappear from the city like her mother had run away from her home? "I must keep my wits", she thought, and went to the closet to retrieve the strong box. The sun had now fully risen. It was the dawning of Isabella too.

Behind the strong box was another box, she did not recall having ever seen. Placing both boxes on the table she began perusing the contents of the strong box first. Sure enough there was her birth certificate, some insurance papers, a bank account book and buried deep in the bottom under a lot of other papers she was going to have to sort through was a marriage license.

The bank account showed $729.53 as a balance. The insurance papers revealed a policy worth $1000.00. Her birth certificate did not show anything unexpected, but the marriage license showed a name she had never heard before and that simply had to be her father! Excaliber Laveau. What a strange name. But that was all it said. No date, place and no other signatures. Was this a legitimate marriage certificate? For the first time in her life Isabella had a name. But for now that would have to wait.

Isabella continued to shuffle papers around barely reading them, but making two piles: one for "must read" and one for "not sure what this is". In the other box she found old pictures and newspaper clippings with large headlines that read, "VOODOO PRIEST SUSPECTED OF MURDER" and another one in a smaller headline in the middle of the page that read, "Marie and Excaliber." She squinted at the picture under the headline to see if their faces looked familiar. This article she read twice.

The clippings were old with time and crinkled badly, but she was able to make out the jest of the story. Apparently it was referring to Marie Laveau, the high priestess of a cult that existed in the Quarter many years ago. She had heard stories about this voodoo queen and had passed what was supposedly her home on Bourbon Street many times. As the story goes, she had been born in New Orleans a free Creole lady who was a hairdresser to the affluent ladies of the city. The rumor of her witch-like behavior was exaggerated over the years by the fine ladies she attended. Whether her power was true or false, she did have a hold in the community as someone you did not offend. Her husband Jacques Paris had died under unexplained circumstances back in the 1820's. People that still believed in her powers would visit her grave in St. Louis Cemetery #1 and draw three X's on the tombstone in hopes her spirit would grant a wish.

The man known as Excaliber in the clippings she was holding was either married or a relative of some sort to Marie. His last name was the same. He was described as a tall man, who rarely spoke to anyone and was generally seen alone walking the streets of the French Quarter dressed in black. He wore a black fedora in the picture that covered most of his face, but even in the old picture Isabella was looking at she could see that he had piercing dark eyes that would scare anyone he stared at directly.

From the facts in the articles she was able to ascertain that Excaliber had been picked up by the authorities leaving Marie Laveau's home right before dawn. They had taken him in for questioning in the murder of Jacques Paris. With no established address or means of income, the authorities had difficulty in holding Excaliber for more than 48 hours, and were unable to continue the interrogation. He left the station with a warning that he would be watched closely.

Isabella desperately wanted to find out more about this Excaliber since that was the name on the marriage certificate that also bore her mother's name. How could there be a connection between the two of them with so many years having past? The name was so uncommon. The timing simply couldn't be. And yet she held the clippings and the marriage license in her hand.

Isabella now turned her attention to the small stack of pictures. Most of them were of her as a baby. There was a picture of Marta in her teen years and Isabella was struck by how beautiful her mother had been at that age.

There was a picture of a group of ladies, perhaps as many as a dozen women all standing together in such close proximity that it was impossible to count them. But it was easy to see that they all resembled one another. Each had long dark hair and dark eyes. They were dressed similarly in tent like flowing dresses and all wearing a lot of jewelry. She turned the photo over in hopes of some explanation of who they might be, but alas the back bore no information.

Another picture was of her mother facing the camera, with a very tall man dressed in black wearing a hat and his back to the camera off to Marta's side. Nothing was written on the back of this photo either.

The next picture she picked up gave her a frightening start. It was a picture of a snake! It was a close up of a white snake with huge eyes. She had never seen a snake with eyes like that in any picture book. On the back of the picture it simply said Zomba.

When the telephone rang, it startled Isabella. She sat very still for a moment and decided to let it ring. Then she decided she had better answer it only to find out it was her school calling to find out why she had not attended classes.

"I'm sorry Mr. Dyer, I should have called. I'm sure you heard the news about my mother and I've been very busy answering questions and helping my aunt make arrangements for my mother. I probably will be going home to Vermillion with my aunt under the circumstances and won't be coming back to school. What do I need to do?"

Mr. Dyer had not heard about Marta and became soft spoken and sympathetic in his instructions as to what Isabella needed to do to get her grade transcripts and such. Isabella had no intention of returning to school and following his procedures. She simply did not care about any of that any more. She had much more pressing issues to deal with than her education.

So far everyone was buying the "aunt" story and that was buying her time. Time to get her mother buried. Time to get a job. Time to find out about Excaliber! But first she had to deal with Officer Culotta who was pounding on her door again.

Chapter **THREE**

The Funeral and The Future

Isabella was so very grateful to the owner and the employees of The Pearl where Marta worked for coming to her aid in finding a funeral parlor and assisting with the costs. It was to be a very simple funeral. One that would hopefully not draw attention to the accident or her.

The day began in bright sunshine, but dark clouds began to hover on her way to the funeral home. It took a trolley and two buses to get there, but she was lost in thoughts and the time past quickly. Dressed in her best grown- up finery, Isabella sat with her head down and not looking in any direction. She missed her mother and still there were so many unanswered questions.

Officer Culotta had little to report to her about what had happened. Some of the witnesses had been questioned but it all happened so fast that no one got a very good description of the driver or car. All they could tell was that it was a big black car with tinted windows and traveling very fast. There was no evidence that the car had even applied its brakes for there were no tire tracks.

Isabella could not imagine that her mother had an enemy that would go to such lengths as to kill her on purpose. There were many questions about her mother brought on by going through the boxes in the closet and there were things she did not understand. Primarily she wanted to know about Excaliber. Was he her father? Nothing more in the papers or pictures seem to add up or give her even a direction to go in to find any answers.

Walking the three blocks from the bus stop to the funeral home, Isabella could sense that someone was following her. The clouds had gotten darker and it felt like rain. She picked up her pace for both reasons.

She entered the funeral parlor just as the sky opened up. She turned at looked back at the entrance to see if someone had indeed come in after her, but no one was there.

The funeral director approached her with his condolences and showed her the way to the small reception room. There were only two people there. Officer Culotta and Marta's friend and boss. Sasha approached Isabella with arms wide open to give her a hug, while Officer Culotta held back.

"You poor girl," Sasha whispered, "are you doing okay?" Isabella looked up at

Sasha's warm brown eyes and gave her a weak smile. "Yes, I'm fine," Isabella replied. "I can't thank you and the other ladies enough for helping me and giving Mama this. I don't know what I would have done without you," Isabella said and for the first time tears began to fall.

Sasha handed Isabella a handkerchief and as Isabella wiped her tears, Sasha told her that following the cremation she was to come with her to the Pearl for something to eat and she wanted to talk to her about a job. That brought a slight smile to Isabella's face and together they walked into the parlor for the ceremony.

Isabella sat in the front row with Sasha seated behind her. In the back of the room Officer Culotta took a seat near the door. Everything was very quiet until the organ began to play a song that Isabella recognized but did not know the name. Then a man she did not know and had never seen before came through a side door and asked them to pray a silent prayer for Marta. The rest of what the man said meant nothing to her and she had trouble concentrating on his words. Then he turned and left the room through the same door and Isabella just sat there with Sasha's hand on her shoulder.

A brisk wind rushed through the room and they turned to notice there were several women standing in the back of the room. Officer Culotta was gone and replaced by all of these women that Isabella had never seen before. They were all dressed in flowing dresses of the same color with hood type thin veils over most of their faces.

They just stood there. No one spoke. Isabella rose to walk toward them and just as quickly as they had appeared, they began to practically float out the door. All but one.

The remaining woman stood her ground as Isabella got closer. Now Sasha was at Isabella's side.

"Can I help you," asked Sasha?

"I've come to pay my respects and to give the young one this," the woman replied. She reached out her hand and in it was a small silk bag which she put in Isabella's hand. "What is it," asked Isabella?

"Open it in private. You might not understand at first, but trust in it. It will help you in the future."

"Who are you and how do you know my mother," asked Isabella?

"It will all become known to you soon, my dear, and we will meet again." Isabella noticed an accent, but could not tell what it was. It sounded Russian, not the French, Spanish or the dialects of the Quarter's Cajun she had become accustomed to over the years. "What is your name lady," Isabella asked? But the lady did not answer and instead turned and walked out of the room and Isabella watched as she went out into the pouring rain.

The funeral director handed Isabella the urn containing her mother's ashes. It was so small and pewter in color. Sasha took it from her hands and guided her out of the funeral home and into a waiting taxi cab. They rode in silence to the Pearl.

Once Isabella was home, she locked the door, sat at the table and stared at the silk bag. She could feel there was something in it, but had not opened it as she was instructed. The storm had passed and the sun had come back out. A strong sunbeam seemed to dance on the silk bag. She picked it back up and held it in her hands. Then she began to untie the small drawstrings that were tied in a knot. The first thing she pulled out was a slip of paper that appeared to have a poem written on it. She began to read aloud:

THE RUNE

Evil and goodness are upon this earth

Some can be determined at their birth

Use these bones to help you find

The wisdom and truth of your mind.

The bag now wide open she reached back in and pulled out two bones. They were as white as anything she had ever seen. They seemed to almost glow. Then she reached back in and pulled out two more bones, but these were darker, almost brown. They looked like chicken bones to her. Holding them up to the light she noticed there were perfectly formed holes in varying places on all of the bones. She held them to her nose to smell, but they had no odor. She was totally confused. There was no explanation other than the poem. She placed them back in the silk bag, retied the knot and put them in the drawer where she kept her mother's tarot cards.

Isabella sat back in the easy chair and recounted the day's events. She placed her mother's ashes on a side table and now returned to pick the urn up and speak to it as though her mother could hear her, "Mama, I don't understand anything. I'm so confused and scared. What happened to you? Who were those ladies? What is this bag of bones and what am I suppose to do with them? Why did you leave me?"

Now Isabella cried. She sobbed for the first time since her life had changed so drastically. She missed school. She missed Marta. The only good thing in her life was that Sasha had given her a job at the Pearl and she was to report for her first day in the morning. It would be barely enough of an income to live on, but at least it was something. And some place to go. But she knew that her life was going to have to amount to something other than waiting tables at the Pearl. She was going to have to look for another job, maybe a part-time job to help out with expenses. She was going to have to continue to lie to people about her age, who she was and what she could do. She was grateful that Officer Culotta did not ask where her aunt was. That was a lie that was going to get her into big trouble and she was spinning such a web that it haunted her. "I must come up with better stories and answers if I'm going to make it alone," she thought.

Feeling more confident and relaxed after a good cry and being fed well at the Pearl, Isabella took her uniform that Sasha had given her out of the plastic bag to try on after a good soaking bath.

While in the tub Isabella laid out a plan. I'll put as many hours in at the Pearl that Sasha will give me, I'll find a part-time job, get the bills all in order and go to the bank to settle accounts and get things in my name. I'll need to find someone in the Quarter to give me a fake ID…that shouldn't be too difficult to find someone….and then I shall begin finding out about Excaliber. I know my way around a library better than most and Mama always said I was a good problem solver. I can do this. I can do this. I can do this.

The first week working at the Pearl was difficult. With trying to learn the menu, how to serve customers, and even sometimes working at the cash register, her stamina was tested. Sasha had scheduled her for thirty hours that first week and she was exhausted. Her feet hurt. Her back hurt. And dealing with some of the natives and tourists at the Pearl could be exasperating. Sasha had pointed out if she smiled more her tips would be bigger, but for the moment she was just trying to get the orders right and that took a lot of concentration.

She hated her uniform. It seemed as though one day she was flat chested and the next those breasts had exploded into double D's. It made buttoning up the front nearly impossible and it kept coming undone. Sasha gave her a larger uniform, but it was so big everywhere else that she looked like a slob.

"We can't have you looking that sloppy, so go back to the original and just wear a T-shirt underneath it," Sasha told her, but even with the air conditioning in the restaurant, the kitchen was always steamy hot and it only made Isabella sweat much more. "Can't I just unbutton the first two buttons Sasha," Isabella asked? Sasha gave her a frown and then agreed saying she wished she had been so blessed as to have them jugs. "Just don't bend over when you are serving the customers," Sasha said with a giggle. "And keep your hairnet on!"

That was the worse thing. That stupid hairnet. Isabella had also been blessed with beautiful black hair that had grown past her shoulders and was quite becoming, but in that hairnet with it all pulled back she felt she looked like an old lady. With her first paycheck she had bought "sensible" shoes and paid the man in the alley for her fake I.D. She purposely had the picture taken in her uniform so as to look even older than she had told the man to print. "Honey, no one will believe you are 21, cause ya look like you're in your 40's, he announced when she picked it up. "That'll be $200 missy," he said as he held up her I.D. "What, she exclaimed, that's all the money I have," Isabella whispered. "Sorry little lady, that's the price of a lie," he reached out with one hand to touch her breast and the other held the I.D. Isabella stepped back as he was suggesting the price could be adjusted if she was willing to pay differently. Naïve as Isabella was in most matters, she was aware that men could be leeches and usually wanted sex. You simply could not grow up in New Orleans without being aware of all of the hookers, conventioneers looking for a good time and the sleazy bars that promoted with a 2 drink minimum a really good time. Marta had become acutely aware of how much Isabella was developing at a young age and had sat her down for the infamous "mother/daughter" talk. But even Isabella was sure it was not the usual talk. Her mother had explained that pretty girls with big boobs could get anything they wanted if they knew how to flirt and tease. There were many, many men in the world that would pay in many, many ways just to have sex with a young girl, so she should be aware that she was the type that would encourage that sort of thing without even trying. "Just make sure you get what you want, before they get what they want," Marta had told her. Those words were now ringing through her head.

"No sir, I'll pay the $200," she said with confidence and then surprised herself by adding, "and keep your hands to yourself. We have concluded our business!"

Isabella planned on spending what was left of the evening at the library. At least there with books piled in front of her she could sit down and rest her feet.

After a couple of hours she was so very tired that reading was just a blur, so headed for the trolley to make her way home. Tomorrow was another day at the Pearl, and she needed to get to bed.

As time past at the Pearl, Isabella was getting pretty good at her job and Sasha was right about the smiling. Her tips practically tripled that week. Even though her hours had been cut to 20 hours, with the tips she was almost making enough to pay the bills. But there sure wasn't any money left over for things that she needed or wanted and she knew she was still going to have to find a part-time job. It was not going to be another waitress job.

She perused the want ads in the Picayune, but most of them were professional jobs that required an education she did not have, or training she didn't even understand. But there were lots of ads for hotels and bars that needed help in various jobs she might be able to do. So she made a list of possibilities, eliminating anything that was wait staff. The next day was a day off from the Pearl, so she intended to go to her first three picks to put in her applications.

The day was a hot one with steam rising off the pavement from the passing rain puddles. She dressed in her one and only good dress, put on high heels, applied her make-up and made sure she had enough change for the trolley, buses and even cab fare if needed. She double checked she had her fake I.D. and took inventory of her appearance in the mirror. After a quick breakfast, she was out the door to seek employment according to her list.

The day was proving to be unsuccessful. Positions had been filled, she didn't have any experience, she could not type and the only possibility turned out to be a maid in one of the middle-class hotels for minimum wage. Plus she was finding that part-time work was difficult because everyone wanted someone full- time and she wasn't about to give up her job at the Pearl. She owed a lot to Sasha.

While strolling down the shady side of Bourbon Street, the afternoon sun was beginning to wane and she knew it was only a matter of a short while before the street became packed with party goers, drunks, loud music and tourists. It didn't matter that it was Wednesday, because every night on Bourbon Street was Saturday night. The girls were already hanging out in doorways in skimpy outfits. Some of which looked like they couldn't be older than 15, but you knew the way they coaxed the scattered few men that they were old beyond years.

"Not for me, Isabella thought, not in a million years."

Having worked up an appetite, Isabella decided to duck into Tony's for a small plate of spaghetti. While seated at the window, she noticed that right across the street was advertising "**Madame Electra**, **Home of spiritual reader, tarot, palms and expert tattoos**." Isabella had never seen that before, but then again it had been awhile since she had walked the Quarter streets. On a whim, she decided to finish her small plate and pay Madame Electra a visit.

She walked into a small lobby with a door on each side and a staircase leading up to the second floor. The doors announced an escort service on one side and a lawyer on the other. Then she saw the arrow pointing up the stairs to Madame Electra. "This is silly," Isabella thought, but checked to see how much money she had remaining in her purse. And then as if she was not empowered to relent and leave, she found herself climbing the stairs to a door that read Madame Electra.

The over whelming scent of incense hit her immediately. She was aware of a small tinkling sound, dim lights and then a sound of soft music that sounded slightly familiar. Bright red velvet curtains to her left suddenly parted and out stepped a woman that gave her a shock. It was the woman that had come to the funeral home and have given her the bones! "Welcome Isabella, I knew we would meet again," she said.

Chapter FOUR

The Reading

Isabella could not hide the shocked expression on her face at the sight of this woman who had suddenly come into her life, now on a second occasion.

"Take a seat, my dear. I won't bite you. We have a lot to talk about, " she said as she approached the door to lock it.

"Why are you locking the door lady," Isabella asked in a frightened tone?

"I do not want anyone to interrupt us. Believe me, Isabella, you are quite safe. I would never harm you and when you hear what I have to say, you will not want someone walking in that door. Relax, honey. Would you like a cup of tea?" She departed through the curtains and Isabella rose and headed toward the door only to find it was locked with a key that was nowhere in sight.

Isabella took a seat near the door and sat very quietly listening. It seemed like an eternity before the curtains parted and Electra returned to the room carrying a tray with a tea pot, tea cups, all the fixings and a plate of simple round cookies.

"Help yourself, my dear. I baked the cookies myself and they're good. You look scared to death child. Please try to relax. I'll pour the tea." Electra was smiling at her and Isabella watched closely as the tea was poured.

They sat for a few moments just looking at one another. Electra was dressed in that caftan style again, only this one was bright and multi-colored. She could not help but notice Electra's long painted fingernails and all the rings on her fingers. She must have had on a dozen necklaces and the earrings were large loops with little figures dangling from the bottoms of the loops.

As Electra asked how she was doing since the funeral, Isabella noticed the accent again, but this time inquired as to where the lady was originally born.

Electra laughed a little and said, "many, many years ago I was born in Hungary. But I have lived here for longer than I can recall."

"Is your real name Electra," Isabella asked?

"That is what people call me, but we will get to that in a moment. For the time being just call me Electra."

"How do you, did you, know my mother," Isabella was determined to get her questions asked as long as she was a prisoner in that room. She could only hope for adequate answers.

"I can see that you are still nervous and I hope after today and what you are about to learn that we can be friends. What I am about to tell you may be a little shocking, but just know that you can trust me. From now on I shall always be there for you. It's a long story, but hear me out and I will answer any questions you may have. I promise. Now drink some tea child." Electra settled herself into her chair, took a big breath followed by a sigh and began.

As Isabella sipped her tea, she listened to this stranger, but began to relax with the soothing sound of the lady's voice.

"Your mother, Marta, must have been about 14 or 15 years old when we discovered her cold, wet and hungry in the swamps. She had run away from home. My sisters were with me. The ladies you saw at the funeral are my sisters. They became Marta's sisters too."

Isabella interrupted Electra, "that's not true. My mother was always vague about her childhood, but she never ever mentioned any of this. Why should I believe you," Isabella asked?

"Now, don't interrupt me again, girl. You have to hear the whole story and like I promised we can talk about any of your questions or fears." Electra's tone surprised Isabella, but she said she would not interrupt again.

"Marta wanted out of the swamps. She craved the city and she wanted pretty clothes and nice things. Life in the swamp does not include that. It can be hard work and lonely. School was the only thing that Marta had and most of time it was such a long walk to such a poor one room place that she was bored and couldn't stand sitting at a desk. Some of the kids were afraid of her. She didn't have any friends. After hearing her complaints and dreams, we decided that she was the perfect girl to bring into our special world. We taught her our ways. Ways that are passed onto the next girl child, and the next and so on. We told her that if she joined us a girl child would be born to her in the next three to five years. That it would become her duty to teach her daughter our ways. She agreed. Electra poured herself another cup of tea and began again.

"After a couple of years, Marta could not conceive. Oh she got pregnant, but could never carry the child. The sisterhood determined that she could only be a fledgling with limited powers. Marta was a bit of a trouble maker among the sisters, always complaining, being lazy but we could not drum her out because she was going to serve a purpose. Isabella, you are that purpose!"

"Me?" Isabella could not help but interrupt.

"I must continue. You must listen very closely now. Marta was taught some of our ways. She understood the tarot and palms, even got so that she could focus on someone to get a good reading of their soul, but she was so angry with the world that what few powers she had, well, they were cruel. When you were born, Marta showed a softer side. She was always doting on you. A kindness none of us had ever seen made it clear that her purpose was raising you. Then one day, Marta gathered her few belongings, you and what she needed for you and ran away again. It took us a very long time to find her. But by the time we located the two of you, we decided to do nothing but observe and watch from a distance. You two seemed to be making it in the regular world okay, but we all knew that eventually things would change." Electra stood now and walked toward Isabella. "This will be hard to understand and even accept, but trust me, child." Electra pulled her chair closer to Isabella and took her hands in hers.

"You were growing into womanhood. It was time for you to come home. The sisters and I approached Marta and she knew what was about to happen. She fought us when we demanded that she give you back to me. It was time for you to be initiated into the sisterhood. As the high priestess, she could not deny me. But she continued to fight us and she was killed."

Isabella released Electra's grasp of her hands and stood up, "this is bullshit lady and I am not going to believe another word. Let me out of here. I shall start screaming if you do not unlock that door!" Isabella was torn between anger, fear and disbelief.

"I am growing feeble in my powers and I have just a short time to teach you our ways.

You do not have a choice Isabella. You have always been aware that you were different. You are a smart girl. You even predicted Marta's death. You know the tarot. You know you have deep feelings and senses that other's do not. It can be your saving grace or it can be a curse. I am here to help you. You need me. The bones will help."

Isabella was aware that tears had begun to fall from her cheeks. She was now weak in her knees. The tea she had drunk must have had something in it because she was feeling light headed and powerless to stand. She slumped into the nearby chair.

Electra continued. "You know the name Excaliber?" Electra looked deep into Isabella's half shut eyes.

Isabella tried to sit more up right at the sound of that name. "Yes, I know that name. How do you?" Isabella asked.

"Excaliber is the father of only girl children. He is the father of my sisters' girl children. He is your father."

Electra walked behind the curtain once again, calling to Isabella to remain seated.

"Excaliber has a gift for you, but before I give it to you, you must listen closely once again."

Electra held a wooden box in her hands. It was plain except for some sort of carving decoration or maybe writing on the front.

"I went to the library to find out about Excaliber, but all I could find was reference to a sword from King Arthur's court. But in a box at my house I discovered pictures and papers I did not understand. Mother had them hidden in the back of her closet. I never saw them before she died. There was a marriage license with his name on it. Do you know who killed her? Was it my father who killed her? "

Electra placed the box on the table and began again with more startling news.

"The name Excaliber does come from the sword. The name is taken because of his very large penis and the power it possesses. He can only produce girl children, which is part of the covenant he has made to live on this earth. His powers are great. He cannot be denied. All of the sisters are married to Excaliber. Including Marta. But when she could not carry a child, Excaliber wanted her banned from the cluster. He was about to discard her when she ran away with you. I had produced a girl child late in life, but I was unable with all of my duties and my waning powers to raise that child. When Marta stepped up to my duties, the child was given her to raise. You asked my real name. All you need to call me is Mother."

Isabella sat looking at the floor trying to gather her rushing thoughts. "I have so many questions and I am so confused by all that you are saying. And I can't be sure I believe any of this. But one thing keeps crossing my mind. Why me? I am beginning to think that my whole life is a lie...or some sordid joke. Please tell me there is nothing more. I don't think I can take any more."

Electra felt sorry for Isabella, but knew that the whole story had to be told while she had a chance to explain everything.

"I know how upset you must be, but it is important that you understand your past so that you can prepare for the future. I know when I was told of my destiny, I was frightened and didn't want to believe any of it. You may think that this is a curse, but you have to trust me that this is a blessing. But it is power you must use wisely. It can be a danger. It can harm you and many others. I will help you. That is what I am here to do. It has not been easy for me these last months watching you from a distance and knowing your fate. In the next few months we will spend many hours together and all of your questions will be answered. That is my solemn promise, Isabella." Electra was saddened by the look of desperation on her child's face.

Electra poured Isabella another cup of tea and pushed the cookies closer. Isabella refused.

"It is time to tell you things that will certainly scare you, but we must continue. When we found you in the city, Excaliber had also known of your where about, but had decided that before he approached you, it was my duty to prepare you. Your initiation was growing near and he was sure you knew nothing of your fate. Marta had seen him a couple of times lurking nearby and was surely planning to run away with you once again. When I cornered Marta she made it clear she was not going to give you up and that she was calling the authorities. We can not have that. We must keep away from any police trouble. Our vow of silence beyond our society is prohibited by death. And death can come in many forms. As to who ran Marta down with that car on Canal is anyone's guess. It was a deliberate action taken by great powers that control many. Was it Excaliber? I doubt it when all he has to do is wish it and it will happen. In the next several weeks or so, you will be presented to him. You will be with him for ten days. There are things you must learn before he calls for you."

"I've heard enough. I want to go home," Isabella sobbed.

Electra now was stern and her tone was no longer sympathetic. "You can leave when I say, but not yet. There is more for you to know and you are going to listen to me. Your life may well depend on it. So stop whining and pay attention. During that ten days you will not know where you are and you will be unable to escape. You will be fed and clothed, but not in those school girl clothes. You will assume the caftan that we wear. You will perform sexual activities with Excaliber and hopefully conceive a girl child. That is your initiation and you don't have any choice. It is our way. It will be your way. It won't do you any good to fight what will happen because his power will be that you co-operate. He will teach you how to please a man. He will teach you how to get your ways when the time is right. He will teach you when to act insecure and when to seize any opportunity. You will be tested before released. And you may find you do not want to leave him."

Isabella now looked upon Electra with less fear and a more intrepid stare. "If I am going to be all that powerful as you say, what makes you think that I won't use these unholy powers to destroy all of you?"

Electra threw her head back in a guttural laugh. "Oh youth, stupid youth. You think you know everything, but even with all of this knowledge I have given you, you will think you can do something about it, like destroy something that has gone on for centuries. When you leave here and are sitting alone contemplating all of this, you had better remember one thing….you have no choice in this matter. Your destiny was determined long, long ago and you will be the better for it to learn, observe, listen and do as your told."

With that statement Electra went to the table and picked up the wooden box.

"In this box is something that will put the fear of all things holy and unholy in you. It is a gift from Excaliber. You will be allowed to possess it only after we have met every day until you are called. During that time I will show you many wonders. We will see how good you are with the tarot and the palm. We will begin with the bones. We will watch the eyes for approval."

Electra reached inside the box and pulled out a large sealed Mason jar that contained two large eyes floating in the air of the jar. There was no liquid. The eyes looked right at Isabella. As she looked back at the eyes, she was not fearful, but instead immediately felt a relief and for the first time she felt safe.

"These are the eyes of Zomba. When the time is right you will have them to protect you. Zomba is all knowing and powerful. The snake is the beginning of desire, lust, and temptation. He sees all. You will learn how to communicate with Zomba and he shall be your best advisor in all things. But meanwhile he will remain with me until your first training is completed and you have been initiated into our society. Do you understand?"

Isabella kept staring at the eyes but nodded yes. "What am I suppose to do next," Isabella asked?

Electra now smiled at Isabella and answered, "You are to come here every day at 5:00 p.m. We will begin immediately at 5:00. Do not be late. Here is $1000.00. Forget getting another job and tell Sasha at the Pearl that you are handing in your notice to begin immediately. I don't care what you tell her as to why. I know she has been good to you, but that is in the past. Your new life begins tomorrow at 5:00. Money will never be a trouble to you. Do not change anything else about your life. Remain silent and avoid strangers. If Officer Culotta comes to your door to ask any more questions or to check up on you, you find a way to dismiss him. Is that clear?"

Isabella rose from the chair still looking at the eyes of Zomba. "I heard every word....Mother....and I will be here at 5:00. May I go now?"

Electra unlocked the door and opened it slightly. She listened for a moment before opening it wide. As Isabella approached the door, Electra wanted to put her arms about her child for the first time in many years, but drew back a step allowing Isabella to depart. She watched as Isabella began to descend the staircase and then heard the door to the lobby open and close. She then turned her attention to Zomba, picked up the jar and smiled at the eyes. "I think we got our girl back," she said to the snake eyes. She placed the jar back into the box, sat down where Isabella had been seated and felt totally exhausted.

Tomorrow we begin, she thought.

Chapter FIVE

The Lessons

After spending a fitful night trying to digest all that had occurred at Electra's, Isabella arose to another humid and hot day in New Orleans. The first thing on her mind was how was she going to tell Sasha that today was to be her last day at the Pearl? A voice inside her head kept telling her she really did not have a choice and that regardless of Sasha's comments, and perhaps even her anger, she had to quit her job at the end of her shift.

When she arrived at the Pearl the first thing that Sasha noticed was that Isabella was not dressed in her uniform.

"Why aren't you dressed," asked Sasha? Isabella hung her head and presented the bag she was carrying with her uniform in it. "I'm so sorry, Sasha. You have been so good to me, but I can't work here any longer," was Isabella's response.

Sasha frowned and just stood there for what Isabella thought was an awfully long time. They both began to speak at the same time. Isabella had practiced her speech on the one block walk from the trolley and began only to have Sasha interrupt her, "nonsense girl, we are short staffed today and I need you. What do you mean you're quitting? Put that uniform on and get to work NOW!"

Isabella was hurt by the tone of Sasha's voice, but understood how unfair she was being. "OK, Sasha, I'll work until 4:00, but then I am leaving and I can't come back. You have to believe me when I say how much I have appreciated your helping me, but something has drastically changed in my life and I really don't have a choice."

She then went into the back to the employee's restroom and changed into her uniform. When she came out, the other girls were staring at her with a combination of anger, disgust and wonderment at how and why could Isabella do this to all of them. They had befriended her and she owed Sasha better treatment.

The day dragged on with no one but customers speaking to Isabella. She was under such stress that she even dropped a tray of dirty dishes when one of the girls deliberately came out the 'in' door of the kitchen. No one helped her clean up the mess she had made and tears fell as she picked up the broken plates.

At 3:30 Sasha grabbed her arm and pulled her into a corner of the kitchen.

"This is the pay I owe you for the few days you worked this week, but I docked you some for the dishes you just broke and because you are leaving with no notice. I am hurt by your lack of consideration. Marta would have given you a beating for your behavior. I don't know what is going on with you, but you had better not show your face in my Pearl again. Don't come back. You are not welcome here after all we have done for you. Leave your uniform in the back and go!"

Isabella decided to walk the blocks to Electra's hoping that the warmest rays of the sun would soothe her heart. She arrived at the lobby a few minutes early and slowly ascended the stairs to Electra's door. Just as she was about to turn the knob, the door swung open and there stood Electra beaming like the Cheshire cat.

"Right on time, my dear. Very good. We can begin immediately"

Isabella took a seat across from Electra and said, "this has been a dreadful day and I have you to thank for it."

"Well, things will look more promising soon. Now let's begin with the tarot and see what you know."

Electra handed Isabella a red velvet pouch and sat back to watch what her protégé' was about to expose as to her knowledge of the cards.

Isabella opened the pouch and using only her left hand as Marta had taught her, she began to move the cards about and then lay them out in the Celtic Cross. That spread was the one Isabella found to be the most difficult to read. She hoped to be a poor student and therefore perhaps Electra would be disappointed. She would feel comfortable in that position for she was used to dealing with it the whole day.

But instead of the cards confusing her, she felt a strange attraction to the cards she had never felt before and did a perfect reading of Electra. "Try another one, " Electra told her and Isabella proceeded with a Pyramid spread and then the Horoscope spread. Never before had the cards revealed themselves in such an intense fashion and never before had Isabella felt so self- assured in reading them.

"I'm impressed. Marta has taught you well. Are the cards warm in your hand?"

"Yes, yes they are. I've never felt warmth from the cards. And it's as though they are speaking to me in my mind. I knew what I was saying was the truth. How is that possible, when always before they felt like just a game to me?"

"That is why we are going to meet each day. I need to observe your powers increasing and find out exactly what we need to do to make them reach a climax. You are now beginning to *feel* the power and before we are through, you also will know who you truly are and need to be, Isabella. Your life is on a threshold of your destiny. Do not fear it. Embrace it. We have only begun."

For the next two hours Electra and Isabella sat very close to one another while they spoke in low voices. Electra had placed the Mason jar of Zomba on the table next to where they sat and both of them with each revelation would look at the large eyes in the floating jar to see an expression of approval.

Electra explained the bones. Each of the bones has holes in them in very specific places. The holes cannot be touched by your hands, but instead after they have been dropped from the bag can only be examined using these sticks. Place one stick in one hole to move it about. Place the other stick in one hole of the other bone to move it about. Feel the power of the bones as you examine them. The darker holes expose more than the white ones. The bones will not reveal as much as other things you will use, but they are a good back up if you should come to a question that seems undefined or confusing. Learn to trust what your instincts and the bones tell you.

"Now let me see your hands, palms up." Electra said. Isabella complied and as Electra took both hands in hers, she sat very still with her eyes closed and remained silent.

"Now you take my hands in yours and do not say anything until I speak again, understood?"

"Reading palms is the easiest of our trade. Peoples' hands reveal not only life lines, love lines, but the callus on them and the shape of the nails give you insight to their personality. The left hand is the personal and private side. It can tell you the person's hopes and dreams. The right hand shows how they present themselves to the world they live in. If the hand is small it can show that the person thinks big, or thinks big of themselves. A person with a large hand is a curious person and is more mental. If the fingers are short, they are quick to make decisions or to loose their temper. If the fingers are long, they procrastinate and have to think every little detail through, often causing them indecision. Because they are too sensitive they can make wrong instincts work against them. Even the length of the nail gives an indication as to how they treat others. For example people with long nails are more giving. They have a tendency to put others first.

"Ah yes, the hands tell us a lot about a person. If you are looking into the eyes, or the soul of the person and you are holding their hands in yours, you will be able to help almost everyone that confines in you. Your power will be such that just doing those two things will make a difference in their lives. But you must remember that such power comes with a price. One you must temper at all times and never give into the temptation to tell a person something that will cause them harm. For your words to them will become not a choice, but a command. Just as you have done as I have told you to do, you will direct others. For did you feel as though you had a choice in accepting all that I have told you? No, my dear, it was my command." Electra sat back in her chair and took a deep breath.

Isabella could tell that Electra was growing tired and weak. She went through the curtains into the back room to see if there was some additional tea. Because Sasha had been so angry with her, she had not eaten anything at the Pearl and felt weak also, but from hunger. Her mind and her senses were on overdrive, so feeling tired had not entered her body or mind. Isabella hollered from the back room, "can I fix us something to eat, Electra?" When there was no response she returned to find Electra had fallen asleep. Wondering whether to wake her, she sat back down and listened for a moment to her stomach growling from lack of food.

As Electra began a slow murmured snore, Isabella decided that it was time to go, but wasn't exactly sure whether she had been dismissed. That is when she decided to go back into the small kitchen and look for something to eat. There were unmarked jars of what appeared to be food, but unable to distinguish what anything was, she found butter and bread and fixed herself a sandwich, and returned to the outer room with a fresh pot of tea. She sat staring at Electra quietly eating her butter sandwich and two cups of tea. She looked at Zomba and asked allowed, "Is she okay? Is this okay?" Zomba smiled. Isabella thought to herself, those eyes communicate with different expressions and I think it likes me!

After about a half hour of sitting there, Isabella decided to wake Electra. With the smallest of nudge on her shoulder, Electra opened one eye and looked at Isabella with such directness, that it startled her. "Sorry to wake you, but are we through, can I leave, or is there more to do?"

"There is so much more to do, so much. But perhaps that is enough for today. You may go Isabella, but return tomorrow at 5:00. We will continue. I must sleep now. With that said, Electra shifted her seating and began to fall back asleep.

Isabella grabbed her small handbag and quietly left making sure that the door locked behind her. It was almost dark now as she left the lobby and headed for home. It was her favorite time of the day. The sun had sat and the last glows were lighting her way. Dusk is the finest time of day, she thought.

For the next two weeks Isabella showed at Electra's doorstep promptly at 5:00

p.m. Isabella grew fond of Electra over that time period as they shared many laughs

and many cups of tea. In that same time period Isabella had spent the early morning

hours looking for a new place to live and a part-time job. Even though Electra always

saw to it that Isabella had plenty of cash on her to purchase anything she might desire

or any bills that needed to be paid. Isabella wondered where the money came from,

but decided not to ask. As long as she was always provided for, she figured why

inquire? The money she had managed to save from "her allowance" as Electra called

it was going to come in useful for the apartments she was eyeing. One was a bright

and cheery place on Esplanade and the other on Elysian Fields. Both were partially

furnished and she was excited about buying all that she wanted to make a home for

herself.

Both neighborhoods were eclectic in architecture, and with more trees and

green lands than the Quarter and her old place, so they just felt more homey and with

quiet peacefulness. She decided she would talk to Electra about her choices in

between lessons. Perhaps her mother might have some suggestions. Isabella was

feeling closer to Electra, but had not decided to call her mother yet.

When she wasn't looking for an apartment, she was looking for a job. Having

no success and feeling rather useless, one sunny afternoon while sitting at Jackson

Square she watched one of the so-called psychics that set up their tables and umbrellas

to give tarot card readings to the tourists. Dressed in finer clothes than she had ever

worn before, she approached one of the tables and asked the old lady what she charged for a reading.

"This will be fun," she thought. "Let's see if this old lady knows anything about the cards."

While she was waiting her turn after a young couple who seemed to be mesmerized by what the lady was saying, all the while listening and trying not to laugh out loud, a man approached her politely and asked some directions. He was very handsome and dressed nicely. After she explained how to get to the restaurant he was inquiring about, he asked Isabella was she visiting the city. "No, I've lived here all my life." He then asked her where she worked. "Matter of fact I have been looking for part time employment and not having much luck," she answered. The handsome man gave her a warm smile and said, "I have a confession. I wanted to talk to you and that was my approach. I know where the restaurant is because I own it. You looked so lovely standing there and when you answered me so thoroughly and sweetly, I felt guilty that I was using a pick up line on you. Are you seriously looking for work," he asked?

"Why, yes I really am, but the only things that are available don't meet my schedule. I cannot work past 4:30 because I am a student and have night classes to attend, "she lied. "I am working on finishing college at Tulane."

"Have you ever been a hostess in a club or restaurant," he asked? "You present yourself in the manner I am looking to find for my restaurant. We could make arrangements for you to work the brunch and lunch crowd if you think you might be interested." He reached into his jacket pocket and pulled out a business card and handed it to Isabella. "Why don't you come by at your convenience tomorrow and we can talk about it."

"Next," the old lady called. Isabella realized the old lady was calling to her for her tarot reading and left the gentleman's gaze long enough to say to her that she had changed her mind and wasn't interested any longer.

Isabella then glanced at the card and read, "William Smithers, Owner." The restaurant was on Chartres and only a few blocks away. She had heard of it, but had never been there.

"Perhaps you could walk with me to the *Red Garter*, let me buy you a drink and we could talk right now. You could look the place over…have you ever been in my place….and then you could either say yes or at least think about it tonight and stop by tomorrow."

"Mr Smithers,"she began, but he interrupted, "call me Bill. And what is your name?"

"My name is Isabella," she answered and then continued that the hour would not permit her to meet with him now, but that she would definitely come to the *Red Garter* around 11:00 a.m. the next day.

He extended his hand to shake hers and with another even bigger, warmer smile said he looked forward to her coming tomorrow at 11:00. "I'll buy you lunch, Isabella, so you can see how good our food is, ok?"

Isabella could not help but look at him as he walked away. He turned back to give her a wave and she waved back. She hoped he could not see that she was almost ready to bust with excitement, but then looked at the clock tower and knew she had to scurry to get to Electra's on time.

By the time she arrived at Electra's she was so full of energy and good feelings that Electra's smile turned to a frown. "What is going on with you, girl," she asked?

Isabella had so much to tell her and the words were coming fast and loud. "Calm down, Isabella. Begin again, slower and more detail."

Isabella told Electra about the two apartments and Bill Smithers and the prospect of the part time job. Electra sat quietly and then said, "So many changes so quickly. Don't you have enough going on without making all these changes? How will this work out when you still have so much training and your initiation into our society? I told you not to speak to strangers. You must not tell a soul about what we are doing, do you understand?"

"For the first time in over a month, I am feeling happy. Why do you want me to not get a job and a new place to live? Haven't I done everything you have told me to do without question? You give me all this money and you expect me not to want to do something with it other than buy pretty clothes?"

"I don't mind the clothes because soon enough you will wear the caftan. I don't mind you finding a new place to live, but I certainly am not too pleased with the idea of you working as a hostess in a bar. Too many people will know you. That will not do. I can't forbid you, but you will see that your ambitions and what you say that makes you happy will in the long run cause you problems. We are wasting time and there is much to do today. By this time next week, you will decide on your own that working is not a choice you can make." Electra then brought out Zomba and told Isabella to tell the floating eyes of her news.

Reluctantly Isabella repeated her news to Zomba. The eyes grew narrow and then turned completely around so as not to see her. "You see, Zomba is not happy. You must not defy him. He knows this will not work."

There was no tea today. Electra was all business and Isabella could tell that Electra was unhappy with her. They went through working on the bones, the palm and the cards in lightning speed. Isabella was becoming so adept at working with them, but was very disappointed to feel that in all practices they objected to her touch. The reading of the cards was ominous and confusing. The light heartedness she had felt on arrival had changed to dismay.

"You have proven to be a good student, Isabella, but it is now time to begin testing your powers. I have an assignment for you. Tomorrow before you come, I want you to go back to Jackson Square, find a bench and sit alone. Focus on one person at a time. With what we call "wishing" you will mindfully instruct your subject to do what you are thinking. Keep it simple. Don't take your eyes off of them and command them to do something like pick up that piece of trash. Don't be surprised if it doesn't work the first couple of times, but keep trying. Wish them to do as you are thinking. Do you understand?"

There was no motherly smile. There was no allowance. There was not the friendly goodbye. Electra simply dismissed her, reminded her of her assignment and told her to be prompt at 5:00 with a report of exactly what had transpired at Jackson Square. Then Electra left the room. Isabella stood for a moment and then left.

The next morning Isabella was torn. Should she show up at the *Red Garter*? Walking to Jackson Square to try the experiment that Electra had told her to try, she decided to let the day come as it may. Her confidence may have been wavered, but it was not shattered.

Taking a seat on a bench facing the cathedral, it was early and not many tourists were about yet. The Lucky Dog hot dog vender was just setting up his cart and slowly the artists, performers and tarot ladies were coming onto the square. Isabella focused on the hot dog vender. Then she watched a drunk trying to light a cigarette with a lighter that would not work. After several tries he threw it away onto the cobblestone squares.

Pick that lighter up and try again, she thought. He continued to slouch up against the building, his unlit cigarette still dangling from his lips. He stopped a passerby for a light, but the man ignored him. Then another man ignored him. She "wished" it again, only this time she narrowed her gaze, stared hard at him and thought stronger, 'pick up that lighter and try again'. Just as she was about to turn her attention to someone else, he walked in the direction of where he had thrown the lighter, he leaned down and picked it up! Light this time, she wished. To her amazement, the lighter worked and the man happily lit his cigarette!

Isabella could not contain her laugher. This is easy she thought. And my first try. She focused back on the hot dog vender and wished that his umbrella would topple over. She glared at it, thought hard and just then a gust of wind came down the cross street of the alley and caused his umbrella to fall to one side.

A young couple approached from the Pontalba building walking in her direction. She watched them closely and then wished that he would kiss her. He did! Isabella could not help but be amazed at what was happening. Then she thought, "now girl, slap him." The girl smiled at the man and then hauled off and slapped him. "Oh my God," Isabella said aloud.

She wished for customers that approached the same old lady tarot reader she had seen the day before to walk away. They did. Some young boys decided to please the crowd that was just beginning to linger about the square with their style of tap dancing with bottle caps fastened to the bottom of their shoes. They placed a hat upside down for coins to be tossed and Isabella wished for a woman to put in some coins. The woman walked passed them, then turned around and put a handful of coins into that hat. Then she wished for a man to put in paper money. He did.

Feeling very full of herself, Isabella now wished that Bill Smithers would come walking her way. She gasped out loud when she could see him approaching her from the corner he had just turned. He seemed as delighted to see her as she was to see him. "Let the day come as it may," she said.

"Well, fancy meeting you here. Are you still coming to the *Garter*," he asked?

"Is it 11:00," she asked? "No, not yet. I was just on my way there. Can you walk with me now?" Isabella hesitated for a moment and then replied, "Don't see why not. How about brunch instead of lunch? I'm starved," she giggled.

They walked the four blocks to the **Red Garter**. Bill unlocked the side door and they went inside. Sunlight had not yet filtered into the windows, shaded by the buildings across the street, so he switched on several lights and Isabella was impressed with the surroundings of mahogany woods, the tables set up with linen and crystal, fine china and ornate silverware.

The bar was off to one side and to her right several yards away was the main entrance to the restaurant. Bill hollered to the kitchen that the boss was in the house and a voice came from the rear saying it was going to be a busy day.

Bill led Isabella down a hallway to an office where he told her to take a seat. Then over an intercom told the voice answering that we need two cups of coffee in the office. Within minutes a young man was introduced to her by the name Creepy. He was carrying a tray of coffee, cups and a plate of scones. "Hot from the oven sir," Creepy announced.

"Have you given my offer any thought, Isabella," asked Bill? "Yes, I have. But I've never done anything like this. What would I have to do?"

The next hour was spent with Bill showing Isabella the restaurant, showing her what would be her station at the front desk, how the reservation book was set up in the shape of tables and how many they seated. He introduced her to each employee that was straggling in, explained the intercom system from the desk to his office and to the wait staff's counter and the bar area. Her position called for her to greet customers, take reservations and she understood that each of the waiters and waitresses would appear to escort the patrons to their tables that Isabella had assigned to each. Answering the telephone came second to someone standing in front of her. Bill was strict about that. "Simply ask them to hold and deal with the face in front of you."

Once all of Isabella's questions were answered, they returned to the office for Isabella to see what her schedule would be, sign a work permit and agree to apply for a food handler's license, even though she would not be serving, it was a requirement. She was told where to go in the city to apply and Bill handed her $100 for her license. She was told that she was not required to wear a uniform like the others, but must always appear on the job properly dressed, made up and hair done nicely. "No one would imply you don't know how to dress and what you are wearing now is appropriate."

Isabella could not but marvel at how this handsome man had turned from warm smile to all business. She respected that. And she liked him.

He expected her at work from 10:30 am. until 2:30 in the afternoon. That was going to be just perfect for Isabella. Would she tell Electra what she had done? Not right away. When she saw Electra that day she was sure Electra would be far more interested in how the "wishing" had gone. For now the **Red Garter** was a secret.

Isabella left Bill and the **Red Garter** after a quick brunch in the office of quiche and salad and she strolled down Decatur Street having walked the block south from Chartres. The clouds had set in and the day was unusually cool. She couldn't help but think how strange that was. She had several hours before going to Electra's and decided to stroll and just look about. What she noticed after the weather was that everyone seemed to look her way. People caught her eye and then just as quickly would look away. She looked at herself in a window reflection to see if something was amiss, but alas her appearance was clean and nice. She had reapplied her makeup before leaving the ladies room at the **Garter.** What was the attraction?

She came upon Who's Voodoo Store, a tourist trap full of gaudy souvenirs of masks, voodoo dolls, bottles of potions, rubber shrunken heads, chicken feet, incense burners, and gris gris. Gross looking T-shirts hung by the hundreds and ceramic crosses were everywhere. She had not visited such a store since she was a small child fascinated by all the thoughts of voodoo and myths of past witches that had once prevailed in the city. These stores were for the tourists, not the true Orleanian.

She noticed a young black man in a Rasti hat and braids at the counter. He was reading something and barely looked up. He did not acknowledge her in any way. She browsed through the store picking up several objects including a couple of voodoo dolls, a mask and a pot that was printed with the words gris gris. She replaced each object where they had sat, turned and started to leave the store when the young man started shouting at her,

"Hey what are you doing? What did you do?" When she turned back around each object that she had picked up had burst into flames and he was running around trying to put out the fire.

"Get outta here bitch. I'm calling the cops!"

Isabella frightened by what was happening turned and ran from the store as fast as she could. There was no time to go home, she would be late to Electra's. She made a beeline for Bourbon Street instead. I have to see Electra now she thought and headed for her mother's.

Isabella arrived out of breath, nervous and bordering on shock at Electra's door. She was over an hour early but was surprised to find the door locked. After knocking several times, she sat down at the top of the stairwell and waited. No one came in or went out. She sat thinking about what had happened at Jackson Square with her wishing and she thought about Bill Smithers. She tried to imagine herself working at the **Red Garter** and her mind wandered to what appropriate clothes she had for her new position as hostess. Then her mind went back to what had happened at the Voodoo Store. Then back to the **Red Garter**. How and when would she tell Electra that she had disobeyed her wishes and accepted the job? Then she thought about Bill again. He had been very nice to her and thorough about what her responsibilities were and she had little doubt that she couldn't handle the job.

Promptly at 5:00 Electra's door opened and she stood in the doorway. "How long have you been sitting there, Isabella, she asked? "I came early and the door was locked. Why didn't you answer my knock?"

"What goes on in this place prior to 5:00 is of no concern of yours. Are you ready to proceed or are you just going to sit there?"

Isabella arose, entered the room and took her usual seat.

"Did you perform your "wishing" like I asked you to do prior to going off with that man to the **Red Garter**?" Electra's tone was disapproving and bordered on hateful.

"How did you know I was with Mr. Smithers? Are you following me now?" It was Isabella's turn to sound hateful.

"Let's get one thing very clear. I know everything about you. Where you go, who you see. I even know your thoughts. NEVER forget that. Zomba and I cannot protect you or may not even want to protect you if you continue to go against our wishes. It has been arranged with Mr. Smithers that you will not be working there. He was not happy, but I told him as your mother that you are not permitted to work with the public in any way."

Isabella was close to tears. "You can't do that. I already told him I was accepting the job and I intend to go tomorrow and apologize for your intrusion. Is THAT clear?"

"You have one choice to make right now. We part right now and you are on your own. You have proven that your powers are beyond my expectations at this time. The sisters witnessed your wishing and reported that you were perfect in every test. Up until now, no one in your position has been able to create wishing so quickly which only proves that you are the Chosen and the one that will need so very much more guidance in order to use your powers in an acceptable way. Left to your own devices, you will follow a path to ruin. All that you have been exposed to is only the beginning. It will become apparent in due time what you are capable of, but I fear that if you choose to leave, that in a short time you will be a memory to me. You are closer to your initiation and I have had to contain my pride."

Isabella sat with her head down. She was caught in a trap that was frightening, exciting and full of adventure that promised to be rewarding in all ways. All that she had learned and the confidence she felt she knew was directly attached to things Electra had taught her and now she was faced with throwing it all away. With a deep sigh, she finally spoke, "So it is all or nothing? Isn't there some way that I can at least pretend to have a normal life along with all this power you say I have?"

"You know the true answer to that question. In time you will have a near normal life. People will respect you. They will even fear you. You will have the power to make anything you want to happen…for yourself and for others. But for now, you simply cannot be in the public eye. Think about what happened in that horrible store. If you do not continue with your lessons and eventually your initiation, you will not know how to control your power and it will be the end of you. And worse than that, you will ruin others. Choose now, Isabella. We will forego lessons for today if you choose to stay. Otherwise, leave here and do not come back. That will be the only choice you will be permitted to make. Choose now....wisely."

Isabella sat, she stood, she walked about the room. Electra remained seated and very quiet. "I've made a decision. I am not sure that it is right, right for me for I am confused as to who I really am, but I do know that I am different and that something I can't explain is in front of me. It goes beyond all the hocus pocus you have taught me. It is a feeling deep down inside that has somehow made it possible for me to accept all that you have told me. Marta was not my mother. You are my mother. That a pair of eyes floating in a jar has powers that go beyond reality. That there is a group of people that I was a part of before I knew anything that would become my world. I may be young in years, but I have always known that I knew more and have always trusted my instincts. Even when I was in school, my classmates treated me as though they were afraid of me and I never knew why. My teachers always watched me out of the corner of their eyes. My schoolwork always came too easy. When I have allowed myself to think about all that you have shown me, somehow it all makes sense. I still don't understand why, but I know what you say to me is the truth. If I really mean that, then I really do not have a choice, do I? My choice is to stay. To continue."

Electra looked at her with the hint of a smile. She put her arms around Isabella and the two stood embraced. "Come tomorrow at 5:00. Now the hard work begins."

Chapter SIX

Preparing for Initiation

Isabella had chosen the brighter apartment on Esplanade and put down the security deposit and the first two months rent. She was pleased with her decision and proceeded to pack up the belongings she wanted to keep from the old apartment and called a church association to pick up everything else. The new apartment was a vital contrast to the darker side of her life that had now become the norm.

With large windows that overlooked the street in the front and the small balcony that overlooked the enclosed courtyard in the back, she was enthusiastic about her decision. The walls were a neutral color in every room, so she asked the super whether she could paint just the bedroom and had gotten permission to do so. It was fun for her to pick out colors at the local hardware store and had decided on a pale blue.

Isabella's days were spent painting, packing, and shopping. Electra had approved of her apartment from her descriptions, but as of yet had not seen it. Money was never any concern because Electra never hesitated to put wads of $100 bills in her hand several times a week. However, Isabella was growing a deeper concern in why and how could Electra continue to just give her all this money. From what she could see Electra had an unlimited source of money, but how was that possible?

With moving day fast approaching, Isabella decided to ask Electra for some suggestions on how to go about transporting things to the new apartment. She did not have a driver's license and a truck was needed. During that conversation she was going to inquire about the money. Isabella had grown more confident in her relationship with Electra and even though every meeting centered on her lessons and explanations of the powers that Isabella was now more comfortable with, they would pass moments of just talking. They were becoming more than teacher and student, mother and daughter….they were becoming friends.

With the apartment taking shape, the new furniture delivered and the kitchen well equipped, Isabella was going to ask Electra to come for tea when she was all settled. Electra would like that, she was sure.

Promptly at 5:00 Isabella entered Electra's place and took a seat. She waited for Electra to make her entrance through the curtains. When she didn't come out,

Isabella peeked through the curtains and was surprised to see five women standing in a circle.

They turned in unison and looked at Isabella. Out of the center of the circle appeared Electra. The five women stood in a straight line all with blank looks upon the faces. All were dressed in black caftans.

Electra looked quite serious and then spoke, "Let me introduce you to your sisters. This is Salem. She will be spending the most time with you." Salem took a step forward, hesitated, then walked right up to Isabella and stood not one foot from her face. Isabella stood her ground, but was growing more nervous as Salem continued to just stare at her not uttering a sound. Then she stepped aside and another sister approached her.

"This is Karma,"Electra announced. She also came very close to Isabella and stared at her expressionless. Then came Fate, Destiny and Rune.

Isabella could feel her knees growing weak. She felt as though she were being sized for a coffin. "What is going on Electra," Isabella asked?

"You have been doing well with your lessons and it was time for you to meet your sisters. They will play an important part in your life for the next two weeks. They will be prepping you for your initiation. You have mastered all of the preliminary tests; the ones we do for the tourists and clients. Even your "wishing" has grown to a point where we need to execute more involved methods of persuasion. You will be permitted to continue your life as you please except now you will be coming to see me every day at 5:00 as you have been doing, but Salem will be with you at midnight every night for one hour."

The seven of them now returned to the larger room and each took a seat in a semi-circle with Isabella seated in the center opposite all of them. Electra remained standing behind them. "Fate, lock the door."

Electra then went behind the curtain once again and returned with Zomba and placed the jar on the table beside Isabella's chair. Then she returned from behind the curtain carrying a tray with seven small clear glasses and a pitcher of liquid that was a foamy green. Everyone sat very quiet as Electra poured the liquid into each glass and handed one to each of them.

"What you are about to partake in is a ceremony dating back centuries. You must never speak of this to a soul. Do you understand?"

Isabella shook her head yes, but could not find her voice.

Each of them kissed the glass rim and then swallowed the contents of the glass. "Now you, my dear, you must drink from the glass and do not be afraid."

Isabella looked at the glass, copied the sisters and kissed the rim and then in one swallow drank the liquid.

Within seconds the room seemed to take on the green cast of the glass in a slow swirling motion. She could hear voices that sounded as though they were from a distance that grew closer and then far away again. She could not make out what they were saying. It sounded like a foreign language she had never heard before. Then

Isabella smelled what she thought was lavender. She raised her hand to look at it and it seemed as though it had grown three times its normal size. The sounds she was hearing now sounded like singing. No, chanting. She turned her head to look at Zomba who now was glowing and it looked as though he had grown a body and was making his way out of the jar. Bright lights began to appear in flashes all about the room. The flashes were becoming figures…figures of warriors with helmets and swords.

Isabella wanted to speak but still she had no voice. Then she leaned forward and vomited. Salem went to her first. She held her head while Fate applied a cool wash cloth on her forehead. When Isabella felt strong enough to raise her head, she was stunned that the room appeared just how it had before she drank the liquid. The semi-circle of sisters were still seated and Electra was still standing behind them. She looked at Zomba, still confined to his jar with only the set of eyes.

"Isabella," Electra spoke, "you will be fine. The potion affects you strongest the first time, but you will come to desire it, even enjoy it."

Isabella tried to stand up, but could not. She tried to speak, but could not. "Just sit there a moment, take deep breaths and we will begin. The hour is growing late. We have much to talk about."

The clock struck midnight. Isabella was regaining her strength and her voice. She surprised herself when her first words were how hungry she was. Karma laughed out loud but was silenced by a glare from Electra.

Two of the sisters went behind the curtain and returned a few minutes later with platters of food. There were cheeses and breads, fruit and little cakes. There was a large pot of tea. The mood had changed to a much friendlier atmosphere. While they all busied themselves eating, the conversation was now almost cordial.

As confused as Isabella was, she was relieved to feel like herself again and listened as each of the sisters spoke in soft tones to one another about varied subjects. Electra pulled a chair up next to Isabella and sat with a cup of tea in her hand.

"I know you must be confused, Isabella, but all of this in time will make sense to you. Before I can have the sisters take you home we must try one experiment. I want to gage the effects of the potion. Are you feeling up to a test?"

A meek yes was answered. "Then let's begin," Electra announced.

The sisters now all quiet and seated with tea watched Isabella closely.

"I want you to tell me what you think you saw. I want you to tell me how it made you feel. I want you to tell me what you want." Electra used her softest voice.

Isabella took a deep breath and began, "I feel different. I felt sick and then I couldn't speak. I felt weak. I saw flashes of light that became men with weapons. I thought Zomba grew a body and was out of the jar. I smelled lavender. I heard voices. I felt like the room was moving. But now I feel fine. I feel like I have slept for a month. I feel strong. I feel young and old at the same time. I see colors. Bright colors all around me. At first I wanted to go home. I felt scared, but then I felt like I could take on the whole world. Like I was seeing and feeling things I've never felt before. I feel very smart and sure of myself and I don't understand why."

Electra patted her hand. "And what do you wish for?"

"I want more answers. My wish is for more answers."

"One question at a time. Proceed."

"Where does the money you give me come from? Do you ever leave this place? You never explained who Excaliber was and how he will play a part in my life. Are these women really sisters? Are they yours? How does Zomba relate to me?

"That was too many questions, Isabella. I will answer just one right now. The money comes from all sorts of people. They are clients; people I advise. People that owe me for favors and they pay generously. My "wishing" skills have brought me great fortune, as it will you. You will never have a need for money and therefore it will never dominate your life. Greed destroys man. While they accumulate it, it never seems to be enough. Most men will give you anything you want or find a way to get it for you. You will learn how to make men give you anything you want. Tell a man that you wish you had that pretty piece of jewelry and he will get it for you. Tell a man that you need to pay your rent and he will provide it. It all depends on how you ask and what you give in return. Sometimes it is sex. Sometimes it is just companionship. Sometimes it is a good suggestion you plant and watch it grow. The power of persuasion and wishing is a power you need to cultivate. We will help you. Let's say you want something in this room. Anything. Just think about it. Concentrate on it. Someone will bring it to you."

Isabella looked around the room. During her lessons she had been impressed with the deck of tarots that Electra kept in her velvet bag. They had practiced with them for hours on end. She knew they were kept in a drawer in a chest that sat in the corner.

Isabella concentrated on those cards. She just kept thinking, "I want those cards."

To her amazement, Salem went to the chest, opened it and came to Isabella's side holding the velvet bag.

"Is this what you wished for, Isabella?" asked Salem.

Isabella shot Electra a look wanting approval. Instead Electra looked away and Isabella reached out and took the bag. "They are mine now, Mother." she announced.

During the next two weeks Salem appeared at Isabella's door of her new apartment promptly at midnight as Electra had said. She always brought a small vial of the potion and Isabella was instructed to drink it right away. With each dosage the taste was acquired and had less and less effect on her, but she could still tell that it gave her added strength and deeper senses.

Upon Salem's first arrival, she asked if she could look around. As soon as Isabella drank the potion, she escorted her to her kitchen, bedroom and out onto the balcony overlooking the courtyard.

"None of us live this nice," said Salem, almost with a sigh. "I think you must be very lucky to live here."

Salem took notice of the newness of the furniture, the colors of the apartment and how comfy everything was.

"I share a place with Rune and Destiny. We are of lower status and Electra doesn't support us like she does you. We all have to have day jobs, mostly part-time, and have trouble making the rent. I wish this were my place," Salem said.

"Careful, Salem. Don't go wishing for my apartment!" was Isabella's response.

Salem giggled and told Isabella, "I don't have your powers, sister. I'm a lowly one."

Isabella was taken with the innocence in which Salem spoke and looked. Dressed in a pair of slacks and a simple blouse and wearing sandals instead of the caftan, she was younger and prettier than her first impression of any of the sisters.

"What is it exactly that we are suppose to do in these meetings?" asked Isabella.

"I'm here each night to teach you the ways of a woman. It's in preparation for your initiation with Excaliber. He will know upon your first minute of meeting whether you will be worthy enough and it is my charge to make sure that you are. We begin with your appearance. Have you always worn your hair like that? Do you know how to properly apply make-up? Let me see your clothes. By the time we have concluded these meetings you will look, act and play the part of a woman that knows what to do in the company of a real man. So we begin with the basics. We will create a goddess by the time we are through. And with your powers that are growing rapidly, he won't stand a chance." Salem giggled again.

They began with Isabella's long black hair. Having always worn it long and loose or sometimes in a ponytail, Salem expertly applied a wonderful shampoo, conditioner, cut it in a most becoming style to frame Isabella's face better and then used a curling iron to give it luxurious curls.

Isabella took much pleasure in Salem's work and enjoyed the pampering. When she looked into the mirror in the bedroom at the finished product, she was surprised at how different she looked. Then Salem opened the make-up box she had brought with her and began giving her instructions about applying creams and foundations. By the time the eye make-up, powdered blush and lipstick had been applied, Isabella hardly recognized herself in the mirror. She was beautiful.

The transformation had taken up the hour they were to spend together and Salem announced that was all for tonight and that she would return tomorrow at the same time. Meanwhile she instructed Isabella that from now on this should be her appearance.

"Practice will allow you to do it as good as I did, but you must do it every day. The ways of a woman begin with her appearance. No more ponytails. When I come back, this is who I want to see." Isabella stood looking in the mirror with Salem standing behind her holding her shoulders stiffly in front of the mirror.

"I feel wonderful….and quite beautiful. No one ever showed me any of this. Where did you learn to do all of this," asked Isabella.

"I thought I wanted to be a beautician when I was a kid. I suppose it comes naturally for me and with my ability this became my job in the sisterhood. There are times when we all get dressed up and the sisters always have me dress them and do their hair"…Salem's voice began to trail somewhat and she continued that the hour was late and she had to go. "The make-up box is yours. Keep it and I'll see you tomorrow." And like a flash Salem left Isabella's apartment.

Isabella filled the next day by playing with the make-up and admiring herself in the mirror. The curls had begun to wane so she tried her hand at the curling iron. Nothing she did replicated the wonderful job that Salem had done, but she reassured herself that with practice she would do better. She could hardly wait for Salem to return that night.

The tapping at the door at midnight alerted Isabella of Salem's return. Isabella could feel the pure delight at the prospect of having a girlfriend. Not since she had lost Marta did she feel she wanted to be close to anyone. Even Electra wasn't a friend. They had laughed together, but never shared anything about themselves other than Electra being the teacher and Isabella the number one student. Their relationship was based more on respect and fulfilling needs.

"Come in Salem and make yourself at home," Isabella greeted Salem with fresh curls and make-up at the door.

Salem handed the vial to Isabella who now didn't even hesitate to drink it down. This was her third dosage and she was beginning to even like the taste of the foamy green liquid.

"Not bad, Isabella, but a little too heavy on the make-up. That's a common mistake. You'll get the hang of it."

"What are we doing tonight," Isabella asked? "And what is in all those bags?"

"Tonight is clothes. I caught a glance of your closet. All wrong. I brought you some things to try on," she answered. "I bet I got the sizes perfect. We will see."

Isabella couldn't get the bags opened fast enough. There were slacks, blouses, dresses in a big garment bag and another bag held shoes and underwear.

Since Isabella was well endowed, the push up bra became unnecessary. Both girls laughed at the sight of Isabella with her boobs practically under her chin.

Salem explained that a woman feels more like a woman if she has on sexy underwear, so they began there. The slimming girdle was something Isabella balked at first, but trusted Salem and left it on. It wasn't comfortable, but when she slipped on the fine black silk skirt, Salem pointed out how she had to wear a girdle under such fine cloth. The white ruffled blouse that was to go with the skirt had a deep neckline that showed off Isabella's breasts. They decided on a pretty pink bra instead.

"I can't wear those shoes," Isabella exclaimed. "Those heels must be four inches high!"

"Nothing shows off a woman's legs and ankles better than a stiletto heel. You can't wear gym shoes with that outfit, now can you?"

Isabella stumbled and swayed trying to walk in those shoes. "They hurt,"

Isabella whimpered.

"You'll get used to them. That's what you need to practice doing. Walking. Up and down stairs, on different surfaces, just walk until it feels natural. Wish that you were gliding on air. Just wish it." Salem couldn't help but admire her product named Isabella.

So trying on more clothes that Salem had brought and walking in the high heels is how Isabella spent the next day. And wondering what Salem had up her sleeve that night.

When Salem arrived empty handed at midnight, Isabella couldn't hide her disappointment. Salem seemed more serious than usual and Isabella was about to ask if everything was okay when Salem announced that they had to get down to more important matters. Salem handed the vial to Isabella who drank her potion immediately and then turned to hear Salem say, "Electra says we are having too much fun and this is not fun business. She reprimanded me and gave me strict instructions to stop playing and instead start teaching you what you really need to know." Salem was not as friendly.

Isabella had applied her make-up, done her hair and was wearing a revealing jumpsuit in pink velvet. She had taken extra time so as to appear to Salem that she was learning, but now she did not feel pretty or comfortable in Salem's presence.

Salem took a seat in the recliner, but sat up very straight. "I can see you dressed for me. You look very pretty. And the heels are no longer hurting? So now walk for me and let me see if you look more confident."

Isabella did as instructed. She walked the length of the room, turned and walked back to where Salem was sitting. Salem sat watching expressionless. Isabella sat down on the couch across from Salem.

"We were having fun. Isn't that allowed at all in this sisterhood? I never had a sister before. I like you and I thought you liked me. Why are you so different? I don't have any friends. Electra seems to go ballistic if I even talk to anyone. She says I have to keep to myself all the time. You are the only person that acts like my friend. I need a friend. I'm lonely," Isabella bordered on a plea.

Salem's expression did not change. She sat for a moment looking at Isabella noting that she was about to cry.

"I am sorry, but there is no way we can be friends. With the position you are about to take and what you are about to embark on will not permit our friendship. Electra was right in scolding me. This is the only life I've known and it would be impossible for me to survive without the society's blessing, so I must obey. So tonight we go down a path that you have to trust me, but do not think of me any longer as your friend. Understood?"

For the next hour, Salem instructed Isabella to walk, sit, stare and only speak single words. After that Salem told Isabella to go into her bedroom, strip down naked and lay on the bed.

At first Isabella started to refuse, but the look Salem gave her and her instincts told her to do as she was told. A few minutes later Salem entered the bedroom, turned off the lights and lied down beside Isabella.

"Don't be frightened. Listen to my words and do as I say." While Isabella lay still, she could tell that Salem was beginning to remove her clothing. Isabella became nervous. Her body stiffened. At first the two of them lay very still and then Isabella felt Salem's hand touching her breast. Then the hand followed the contour of her body down to her thigh. Isabella wanted to get up, but found that her body was not reacting to thought but to deed. The hand was caressing her thigh while the other hand reached for her face. Then she felt Salem kissing her. As much as Isabella wanted to run, she did not seem to be able to move.

"It's the potion, Isabella. It's working. Try to relax and enjoy my touch. This is the beginning of the teachings of sex. You are a virgin, yes? Excaliber wants you as a virgin, untouched by man, but knowledgeable in the ways of sex. How else can we achieve such a demand than to perform your teachings with a sister?"

Isabella's mind began to wander into an unknown world. While she was very aware of what Salem was doing, she was powerless to react. Instead she began to feel warm. Salem told her to turn on her side facing her. Now she was to suckle Salem's breast. She was instructed to reach between Salem's legs and to place her fingers inside Salem's vagina. As Isabella obeyed each command, Salem was doing the exact same thing to Isabella.

Isabella felt her body now loosening and a rhythm of humming or drumming was swirling through her head. She felt her body giving to and fro to that rhythm and succumbing to the gentle touch of Salem. Salem was seeking her anus with her hands, all the while kissing her on her body. Then Isabella felt Salem's lips on her vagina. A rush of adrenaline caused Isabella to give out a muted moan. While she writhed at the touch and moaned at the feelings of pure pleasure, Isabella uncontrollably peed.

Salem backed away and sat up. Isabella began to cry. She was both embarrassed and excited. Salem reached over and turned on the bedside lamp. After Isabella's eyes adjusted to the light, she could see Salem sitting beside her on her shins smiling.

"That's enough for tonight, Isabella. Are you all right? You have a magnificent body. Excaliber will be pleased after some more lessons. I am going to get dressed now and leave. I'll be back tomorrow at midnight."

Isabella got up from the bed and stared at the pee she had left behind. She quickly grabbed the sheets and bundled them. She then grabbed an old shaggy robe and covered herself from neck to foot. She was shaking. She felt dirty and wanted to shower.

The next morning Isabella was in a strange mood. Although she enjoyed Salem's company, things had changed. She was torn between wanting her to return that night and perhaps not answering the door. As she busied herself in the apartment cleaning, doing laundry and then some grocery shopping, her mind kept going back to what had happened with Salem. She realized that she had never had a sexual encounter and therefore had nothing to base an opinion on in regard to how she felt. Boys had been attracted to her, but always seemed afraid to spend any time with her beyond a pleasant hello or conversation in school about homework. The only man that ever acted interested had been Bill Smithers at the **Red Garter**. She had concluded that it had been strictly business and Electra had put an end to that immediately. She had felt a strong attraction to him, but with Electra's interference she decided to put him out of her mind and simply accept that the attraction was not mutual. At any rate, she was not in a position to even pursue it. Deep down she wanted to take that job and just be a working girl without any special treatment in spite of the fact she knew that sort of a life was not going to be possible. With everything that was happening to her, she could not help but think about what her life would be like if Marta had lived, Electra had not come into her life and if she had not got all caught up in this society that she was being groomed to lead.

Promptly at midnight the familiar tapping at her door sounded. Isabella stood frozen on the other side of the door, but after some hesitation decided it would be best to open it. There stood Salem as she expected holding more bags she hoped were clothes or make-up or anything that would allow them to return to their more pleasant meetings.

"Tonight, we learn more about the man," Salem announced.

Salem reached into the bag and handed Isabella a soft, rubber like object with ripples on it.

"What is this," Isabella asked?

"It is what is referred to as a Dildo. It's an approximation of a man's penis. Tonight's lesson is all about the man's sexual organ and how a woman should touch and fondle it. It is used by women for their own sexual needs when the real thing is not available. And that happens for many different reasons. But for you, tonight, it is a teaching tool. Women use them to penetrate their vaginas and stimulate their own orgasms. We however will not go that far because it is important that your hymen be left intact and you remain a virgin for your meeting and further teachings with Excaliber. I also have the equivalent of a man's testicles. You need to know how to properly kiss the balls." With that last statement, Isabella could not help but see the smile that Salem was trying to suppress.

Salem reached back to Isabella to take the Dildo from her and then when she handed it back to Isabella it was vibrating. "Not all of them do that, but this is the top of the line. It is true to the feel and the touch." Now Salem was smiling.

Isabella on the other hand felt the mixed emotion of confusion and it was bordering on disgust. "Don't look so worried Isabella, it won't bite you. It is yours to keep and use in the way it is intended later... much later. But for now we will learn how to caress it in many different ways."

The two women moved to the bedroom, undressed and lay on the bed. The night was spent touching one another, fondling the Dildo, placing the vibrator in different positions as Salem taught her to do. Salem explained that when a man and a woman are having sex it is truly liberating and should be thought of by the woman as an adventure of the body and if he is the right man, it unlocks deep feelings all the way to the soul. Then she reassured Isabella that Excaliber was indeed the right man and that he would teach her so much more about sex.

"What we are experiencing is what they call foreplay. A lot of kissing, but the mouth is a tool just like the Dildo. Here take these balls and lick them, kiss them and fondle them. They are very similar to what a man's testicles feel like. Smell them. There is even an odor of a type that you may encounter."

They continued for about an hour, moving about in different positions and Isabella could feel that she was feeling an arousal she had never felt before. Salem was gentle, but explained that not all sex is gentle.

"Men like to play games with the women they bed. Don't be surprised if he wants to tie you up, or spank you or ask you to act in a certain way. We women are much more in control of the situation then you might think. Unless a man forcibly rapes you, in your mind you must always remember to play their game until it feels as though you are in control. And believe me, when they are weakened by the woman, she is definitely in control." Salem then sat on the side of the bed looking at Isabella as she laid there with a sheepish grin on her face.

"The potion that you drink each night when I arrive helps to relax you and make you more accepting of your lessons. I notice that you do not hesitate to drink it right down now, so you must be getting used to its taste," Salem asked?

"Yes, I think I have grown used to it and although it does not make me feel woozy like it did, I still feel my body reacting to it. I seem to hear, see, feel, smell and taste everything in greater ways, but it wears off and I find myself wishing I had more. Is that common amongst the sisters" Isabella asked?

"Excaliber will teach how to make the potion, so that you can have an endless supply; after your initiation. But for now that is enough for tonight." With that Salem stood up, dressed and as she was leaving the bedroom she turned and told Isabella, "See you tomorrow night."

The lessons were getting easier with each of the next ten nights that Salem came at midnight. More attention was spent on her appearance, her walk, the way she sat, even a lesson in how to serve a man a gourmet meal.

There was more lovemaking, lots of talking about how to correctly smile and laugh with a man. The art of flirting came easy for Isabella. She learned how to look at a person with her eyes saying dirty thoughts. She was turning into a courtesan without being a whore. She still possessed an innocence that Excaliber would find appealing. And their lessons were coming to a close.

It was time for Salem to report to Electra that Isabella was ready for initiation.

Chapter SEVEN

Excaliber

The sweltering humidity had been on the increase with daily rain showers. The tourists were less in numbers as the heat increased that summer. Isabella had performed to Electra's approval and had mastered all that was required of her. She was an expert at tarot, palms, bones and wishing. She had developed a self-confident air about her and had adapted quite well with the help of Salem in becoming now more than just a beauty. She walked with poise, dressed in classic attire and now knew that she caught the eye of anyone that saw her in her daily routine and chores.

As she would now no longer be required to be at Electra's every day at 5:00 and the nightly midnight visits of Salem had concluded, she had more freedom to walk the streets of the French Quarter. She was aware that people stopped as she approached them and stared at her. Sometimes they would smile, while other's dropped their gaze or looked away. She no longer played the game of wishing for unsuspecting subjects to do the maneuvers she wished upon them. Isabella had been tutored on how to control certain urges and thoughts after it became apparent to her that she did indeed possess unspeakable power over people. She filled her days at the library or shopping.

The money that Electra had given her over the last months had amounted to a sizeable bank account and although she did not need to get a job, she felt that it might be what she would do next. Electra had not given her blessings in doing so, but had not condemned the thought either. Their last conversation had left Isabella in a quandary about that decision. The only thing that Electra had said in the past was to avoid everyone and keep to herself. Now she wondered whether she was actually free to be in the public eye and get a job.

Isabella needed Electra's approval or final word on the subject so she decided that day at 5:00 she would report per usual and ask permission.

Isabella walked to the Bourbon Street address as she had done every day now for what seemed her entire life.

She knocked at the door several times, tried the door handle and found it locked. She continued to knock when a man came up the steps and asked if he could be of help?

"There is no one there anymore. Are you here to ask about renting? I'm the building manager and saw you come in. Didn't you notice the For Rent sign?"

Isabella was at a loss for words. She stared at the man she had never seen before and asked where the lady was that had been in that space?

"I don't know where the man is that rented that office space. He paid the rent with cash every month and then last month said it would be available soon. He paid me a bonus to keep my mouth shut. Can't help you, beautiful; don't know nothing."

Isabella slowly walked down the steps into the street feeling lost, confused and disjointed in thoughts. Electra never said anything about leaving. She had always been there. For her suddenly to disappear was frightening to Isabella. And who was the man the manager referred to? What man?

With no particular place to go and feeling less confident about everything, she started slowly walking back home. If people were watching her now, she paid no attention, as she was rapidly thinking in different directions as to what was going on with Electra. Arriving at her apartment door, she felt sick to her stomach. The only thing she could do was bide her time until midnight and hope that Salem would come. Maybe she would have some answers?

Darkness had just begun to fall upon the Quarter. Isabella sat in her recliner staring at a mundane TV program she was not paying any attention to when there was a tapping at her door. She wasn't expecting anyone as it was too late for any deliveries and it was too early for Salem. Cautiously she peered through the peephole in the door and saw Electra. She swung open the door about to burst into tears, but was suddenly taken back by the fact that Electra was not alone. Standing behind and beside her was her sisters. She had not seen Rune, Fate, Destiny or Karma in some time, but set her eyes upon Salem immediately. Salem and Electra were the only ones that had not drawn their hooded caftans close to their faces. All dressed in black they were a sight of forcefulness that would have frightened anyone.

Electra pushed her way through the door with the sisters following. Nothing was said until Isabella spoke up and said, "I was at your place at 5:00 and some man told me you were no longer there. He said a man pays the rent and that he gave notice a month ago that the place would be free to rent. What's going on? Why didn't you tell me you were leaving the only place I know where to find you? Do you know how you frightened me? I am truly angry with you. Explain yourself right now!"

Electra lowered her hood further away from her face and the light in the apartment cast enough light for Isabella to see that Electra was very old. It was as though she had aged 30 years in one day. Electra did not balk at Isabella's tone or harsh words, but instead lowered her chin and looked at the floor. Salem stepped forward and spoke for the group.

"It is time, Isabella. Here is your black caftan. Put it on. We are going to take a little ride."

Isabella hesitated for only a moment, the whole time watching Electra. Electra did not say a word. She would not even look at Isabella. Karma, Rune and Fate went into Isabella's bedroom and returned a few minutes later carrying a suitcase containing Isabella's belongings. Salem had instructed them on exactly what to pack.

Salem then handed Isabella the potion, a larger vial than ever before and told her to drink all of it.

"Where are we going?" asked Isabella. No one spoke an answer.

It was only then that Isabella noticed that Electra was holding the box containing Zomba.

Destiny took the vial from Isabella and helped her adjust her caftan, pulling the hood up over her long black hair. There was no expression on anyone's face, however Isabella thought she detected a slight smile on Destiny's lips.

The seven women then in procession with Isabella in the middle walked out of the apartment. "Make sure the door is locked Destiny," instructed Salem and they all walked into the darkness of the street. Even the lamppost light had been darkened. There awaiting them at the curb was a long black limousine with a driver.

Each of the women entered the limo with Isabella seated between Fate and Salem, while Electra got into the front seat next to the driver. The silence of the group made it impossible for Isabella to speak. She sat with her hands folded in her lap and tried to see where they were going but the darkened windows made it impossible.

As bet as Isabella could figure they had been driving for about 45 minutes and she could tell they had left the city noises and lights. She had no idea what direction they were going. The additional potion had made her relaxed and she fought falling asleep. The silence was deafening.

Suddenly the car came to an abrupt stop. The doors opened and everyone but the driver and Isabella got out of the car. Isabella squinted for a look at where she might be, but the doors slammed shut and she could hear the sound of the doors locking.

The car started moving again, but only for a short while, maybe as much as two minutes. Then the car slowed down to a stop. Isabella sat motionless. That's when the driver turned around and spoke to her.

"Isabella, let me introduce myself," said the driver as he removed his chauffeur's cap. He then placed his black fedora upon his head, but not before Isabella could see his steely black eyes, dark complexion and his black hair graying at the temples. The driver had put the interior light on for his introduction. "My name is Excaliber."

Isabella was sure he heard her gasp. "Don't be afraid, my dear. I have waited a very long, long time for this meeting. We are going to be very good friends. Very good indeed. Now if you will come with me, I will show you where you will be living for a while. I will not leave your side, so you do not need to be afraid. You are perfectly safe."

He then got out of the car, retrieved Isabella's suitcase, opened the door and held out his hand. As she took his hand, she noticed how large it was, however it was almost feminine to the touch. He placed her arm in his and escorted her up a long walkway onto a sweeping porch of a stately manor. As he unlocked the door, she did a quick look about to see if she could identify any of her surroundings. Nothing looked familiar. It was too dark to make out anything but the house that was aglow in light.

They entered the foyer. It was large enough to be a dance floor with beautiful chandeliers and antique chairs. Isabella had seen many pictures of these stately mansions, but had never been in one and was taken by the opulence of what she was seeing.

There was a long double staircase that led upstairs, but Excaliber guided her to the sitting room immediately to her right as he put her suitcase down at the bottom of one of the staircases. She entered the sitting room with its plush carpet; more antiques and fine paintings and tapestries on the walls. The room smelled like jasmine. She saw that on a rare old coffee table between two huge divans facing one another in the middle of the room was an assortment of expensive cheeses, teacakes, finger sandwiches and a carafe of coffee.

"Make yourself at home….this will be your home….for a while," he reported while he poured himself a cup of coffee. "Do you care for some coffee, my dear

Isabella," he asked?

"Am I prisoner here," Isabella finally asked?

"I hope that you do not come to feel as a prisoner," he laughed, "however for a while you may not leave. I don't suspect you could find your way off these grounds and there is danger in the woods and swamps around here. I will do whatever it takes to make you comfortable during your stay. You may find that you won't want to leave. We will be forever connected in a very short time. I know you have many questions as I do, but they can wait until morning. If you are hungry, please eat something. Then I'll show you to your room."

The morning sun was especially bright and sunny with a cool breeze. Isabella awoke, unpacked her bag the rest of the way and slipped into a pair of Capri pants and a loosely fitting knit top. She then tip- toed down the stairs to the massive front porch. She was slightly disappointed to find Excaliber already sitting on the veranda drinking his coffee with a plate of scones on a table in front of him.

"Good morning my belle, did you sleep well?" he asked.

"Yes, thank you. My room is lovely and I do not believe I ever slept in a more glorious bed," she answered.

"Today we begin to know one another. I'm sure you have questions?"

"A list of them," she giggled and batted her eyes at him in a most coquettish way.

"I see that you are a product of Salem," Excaliber grinned. "However, your ways may not work on me. I am not your usual 'dick'- tated man. I think you will find me far more than that. What is your first question?"

"Is Electra really my mother? Who exactly was Marta? And who are you? Isabella had now found her voice.

"That's three questions! But let's begin. Tell me what you know and I'll fill in any blanks. I have all of the answers and now so shall you."

Isabella couldn't stop talking. She told the story of being a student, her mother's hit and run accident, and how she had worked at The Pearl as a waitress and how nice Sasha had been in helping her. She then told how she met Electra and her sisters, the lessons she had learned at Electra's place, and how she understood she was different, but only recently began to accept it. She found her powers to be far more than even Electra had anticipated. She explained that at first she had been frightened of Zomba and drinking the potion but now it had become something she craved. She told him about almost getting a job at the **Red Garter** and Bill Smithers and how Electra forbade her from associating with people and especially Bill and getting a job. She told him about her apartment and how Electra always gave her so much money. She told of her friendship with Salem and how Salem had taught her the ways of womanhood. She finished with going to Electra's place and the man telling her she was gone and then how the sisters and Electra showed up at her apartment and that the next thing she knew she was here.

Isabella was astounded at her candid and personal remarks to this stranger, but for some unexplained reason she was comfortable telling him everything.

Excaliber sat and listened intently to every word spoken. He could see that in spite of her appearance of a woman, she was still just a confused girl. When he stood up, Isabella saw that he was wearing a caftan similar to those of the sisters. His sandals squeaked as he approached the front door and motioned for her to go inside with him, but then returned to his chaise saying, "Today we will fill in all your blanks, answer all of your questions and begin your final chapters in the teachings of the society. You have a very important role to play and I must be sure you are worthy. Electra tells me you are. But you must prove it to me."

Isabella had sat staring at Excaliber, focusing on his intense eyes. It was difficult to figure his age, but he appeared to be not over 40 years. However if he had been the man in the pictures she had discovered in Marta's closet, that simply wouldn't be possible. She decided to ask.

Excaliber smiled, threw his head back with a sigh and said, "I was going to wait a couple of days before we got into all of that, but I guess Electra was right…you are curious and impertinent. Do you see those trees off in the distance? At the foot of each of those trees is a growth of moss-like fungus brought here from the old town at the bottom of Mt.Codrului in the Hungarian Mountains centuries ago. The fungus is the main ingredient of our potion, or what we call "relaxer" and it is what makes it foam and green. One of the things you will learn shortly is how to concoct the potion. Now that you have acquired a taste for it and you know that it can serve you, what you probably do not know is that your body now requires it. We will walk to the trees soon and I'll show you how to harvest it and then help you make your own. I am sure you noticed that Electra looked aged and worn the night she appeared at your door to escort you here?"

"Yes. She not only looked old and haggard, but she was silent and not herself. I don't believe she said a word and THAT is not like her at all," Isabella stated. "And I can't help but wonder where she went when she got out of the car. Is she here somewhere?"

Excaliber's expression changed to a serious frown and he sat up straight in his chair. "Best to forget about Electra. She is not here. She has gone and you will never see her again. Electra's usefulness is over. She no longer takes the potion and the result is what you saw. That would happen to you in time if you would decide to no longer take the daily vial. That is also why you must learn how to make it in large batches and continue it every day. But for now, you are young and beautiful, so no need to worry."

"Does Salem and the other sisters drink it every day too?" she asked.

He decided to ignore her question and instead rose to go inside. While Isabella sat and thought about what he had said, she stared at the mysterious trees in the distance. When he came back onto the veranda, he handed her the vial. She did not hesitate to swallow it.

The day was filled with Isabella proving that the lessons given by Electra had not been in vain. She never stumbled on the bones or the tarots, but when she took his hand to read his palm, it was once again she noticed how soft and feminine his hands were. When she turned his palm up, there were no lines, no ridges, not a single fingerprint. Excaliber could see that Isabella was confused, but chose not to say anything.

She ran her fingers down the front and backs of both hands and then finally said, "I can't read your palm, but the length of the fingers, the nails and the largeness of your hand tells me that you are very virile."

Excaliber pulled his hands away from her suddenly. "Show me your wishing," he commanded.

Isabella had been anxious to show off her powers of wishing and began with small feats. She sat back in her chair, closed her eyes and wished for the overhead chandelier to suddenly light. All of the lights in the entire house came on and shown brighter than usual. Even Isabella was shocked at what happened. Then she wished for the fireplace to ignite which truly caused Excaliber to take notice. There were no logs in the fireplace!

"Well, that indeed is quite impressive, my dear. Now wish for something that you don't think you can make happen."

Isabella thought for a moment. Then a smile came over her face. What she wished for more than anything was that Salem would come to her and be her friend once again.

Without saying a word, there was a knock at the door. Both Isabella and Excaliber were jolted from their chairs. As they stood looking at one another, Excaliber announced that no one was expected. In fact no one was supposed to be on the property. He told her to stand still and be very quiet while he approached the foyer and went to see who was there. Before he left the room completely, Isabella said to him, "I wished for Salem."

Excaliber turned and glared at Isabella. She could tell that he was angry with her.

"You may have proven just how strong you are, but that was a bad idea. Didn't Electra teach you that with that kind of power you have to be wise and think things through before you act? You stupid little girl. You have put your sister in danger!"

Salem stood with a blank look on her face as Excaliber approached the door. He wasn't sure just which one of the sisters it was, but assumed it was Salem because that is what Isabella had wished for and now he was confronted with her at his door. For a moment he thought he would tell her to leave, but then reconsidered and swung the door opened and said, "Isabella is expecting you."

Salem entered cautiously into the foyer. From the sitting room Isabella appeared and rushed to hug her. Still bewildered by the fact she was with Rune and Fate and the next second she was on Excaliber's porch, plus coming in from the bright sunshine, placed a perplexed look upon her face.

"I'm so glad to see you, Salem. Isn't this place beautiful?"

"Isabella, I am not suppose to be here. What have you done?" Salem whispered.

Excaliber stood with his arms folded on his chest and a stern look upon his face. It was the beginning of his and Isabella's relationship and he wanted her to trust him, but this was a bad situation. No one before Isabella had ever outsmarted him and he was both appalled by her actions and yet proud of her ability. No one, not even Electra, had displayed such enormous power at such a young age.

Excaliber was now staring at Salem and began to vibrate his body. He extended his hand toward Salem and pointed his index finger directly at her and announced, "You must leave immediately."

"No, no I want her to stay; she is my friend and I like her," Isabella protested.

Salem stood transfixed and then just as suddenly as she had appeared, she was gone. Now it was time for Isabella to be angry. "Why did you send her away? Where did she go? I think I will leave now also. I've had enough of all of this. I don't want to stay here any longer." It was shocking how strong her objection was and she did not care if it made Excaliber mad.

Suddenly a strong wind slammed all of the doors in the house. The lights that were shining so brightly all went out. Darkness in the mid-day loomed all around the house. The quickness of the mood surrounding them and the air becoming so thick it was hard to breathe caused Isabella to become frightened.

Excaliber ordered her to her room and told her to stay there until he came to get her. She did not question his demand, turned and ran up the staircase to her room where she slammed the door and looked to lock it, but there was no lock on the door. She sat down in the chair beside her bed and watched out the window as the dark clouds began to dissipate and hoped she would see Salem out of her window. But alas Salem was gone.

Several hours passed. Isabella remained sitting in the chair thinking about her life. So much had changed and even though she had never felt more confident in who she was or the fact that she had accepted that she was a powerful person with abilities beyond human, she could not help but wonder what would lie ahead for her.

Excaliber never came to her room. In spite of growing hungry, Isabella chose not to leave her room and remained there throughout the night.

The next day Isabella descended and headed for the kitchen to get something to eat. Excaliber was seated at the table drinking coffee and barely looked at her as she entered. Not a word was spoken between them. She fixed herself some toast and a glass of milk and sat down. They remained silent.

"Today I want answers to all of my questions," she finally broke the silence.

"Today we gather for the potion and you will learn. That is all we do today," he stated.

During the long walk to the edge of the forest of trees, the two never spoke. When they arrived, Excaliber showed her the mossy fungus, showed her how to harvest it and told her that no one should ever be told about it.

"It would not have any effect on those that do not carry the blood, so it would be of no use to them. If you would speak of it and someone decided to destroy it, that would destroy you. So there is no benefit in speaking of our plants. Do you understand, Isabella?" Excaliber's harshness had not subsided over the night.

The day was spent with Excaliber showing Isabella how to separate roots from the moss, how to grind it, cook it and place into special glass jars that looked like jelly jars. When several dozen were full, they were sealed with wax to be stored in a dark cupboard. He then handed Isabella a notebook and told her to record the process and to be sure and date it. This will be your tally and you must keep it religiously. When she put the first jar in the cupboard she noticed that there were hundreds of jars and journals probably containing potion and records. Some were very dusty, but she could see that there were names of people she did not recognize on labels on some of the jars.

"Am I suppose to label my jars with my name," she asked?

Excaliber ignored her question, turned and left the room they had been working in for several hours. Not knowing what else to do, Isabella followed him out.

"Can we talk now," she asked?

"I will meet you in the parlor after a long soothing bath. You should probably do the same. I'll decide what I will answer and what I will not," he said.

The time drew near to dinner and Isabella could smell a great aroma wafting up the stairs. She had bathed, taken a nap and now was dressed in a brightly colored caftan she thought Excaliber might admire. She had taken extra time to expertly apply her makeup and had done her hair in long loose curls. She felt renewed and only hoped that Excaliber's mood had changed to his more charming manner. She was not disappointed.

Dinner turned out to be pleasant with small talk about the French Quarter, her studies when she was in school and a little more history about the great mansion they were living in with its magnificent rooms of antiques.

Excaliber had lived there more years than he could remember. But he didn't always stay there. He spent a lot of time with Electra in the city. He spoke of Electra in her younger days, comparing her to Isabella. He spoke of the mountain countryside of his native land in Hungary. He then offered her information about her sisters and how he was sorry that he had to dismiss Salem. He understood that Isabella did not have any friends, but that it was necessary she remain aloof and distant. It was obligatory since being introduced to the society that she was being groomed to lead. Isabella sat quietly listening to him, gleaning any information she could gather and being almost hypnotized by the melodic tone of his voice.

"Would you please tell me about Marta? And my most burning question is, are you my father? I still don't know how I came to be this person you say I am. I've learned through bits and pieces and my teachings with Electra all of the powers I have. I understand the games of tarot, palm, bones and I see that my wishing powers are very strong, but I still don't know who I am and where I came from." Isabella in all her beauty and confidence still felt naive' and needed more.

Excaliber took a deep breath and began.

"Electra and I decided when you were to be approached. Marta was not your mother. She was a guardian so to speak because of Electra's duties she was unable to raise you. Marta tried to allow you to grow up normal, but we both know you are not normal. Marta would not relinquish you and tried to conceal you from us. She knew that eventually you would be with us, but she fought us. She needed to depart. I made sure that happened. It was I in the car. I wish I could say I was sorry because I know you loved her, but there was no other way. She was about to run with you again. Electra told you she was your mother and biologically she is. But she did not want to raise you and couldn't. Marta had not fulfilled her duties as a sister should….that being giving me a girl child…so her only duty was to raise you. It was that or be banned from the society. So she served a purpose for a while. We had cut Marta's supply of potion. She was a lot older than you thought she was and she created her own doom. All of your sisters have produced a girl child by me. Yes, even Salem. But you will never meet them. There are hundreds of people in our family you will never meet. Don't ever ask me where they are, I will not tell you. But they will serve you in many ways. I am the father of all girl children in the family. I can only produce girls." Excaliber hesitated, dropped his head and then began again, "All except one. There was a boy once."

"Why can you only produce girls and do I understand rightly that I am one of them," Isabella asked?

"My answer to that question is that when I was born of our people I was anointed and it was proclaimed that I could only produce female children. When a son was born, it was decided that he be put to death, but Electra saw my disbelief and joy and used her powers as queen to protect him. I never saw him again, but his life was spared. I was in her debt and she and I became inseparable, ruling the society on all borders and boundaries."

"So you and Electra are my real parents?" Once again the simple question was avoided.

"How do you make your money? I mean what exactly is your job? How could Electra keep handing me large sums of cash when I never saw any means of income from any work? She told me she had clients and people that were generous, but she never told me what exactly she did. Surely it wasn't just from tealeaves, tarots and bones. And it must cost a fortune for upkeep on this estate. How do the two of you manage?" Isabella leaned in for her answer.

"You will never want of anything. Once you have assumed your true position in the society, your needs will be met at every turn. It will never be necessary for you to work. Our people work for you. Let's say you want something and wish for it. We all hear that message. It will keep you from greed. Greed is the one thing that destroys most people in this world. They always want more. But if they could have what they need, and temper their needs to others, the world of the non-society would be kinder to themselves and others. Let me give you a good example: a man drives a full functioning automobile that he enjoys, but he thinks he needs another one. Why? A person gambles to get money for things they need. But they end up gambling the money they have. This need is destroyed by greed of wanting more. Do you know how many people are in charge of the sheep? They will tell you it is human nature. Bullshit. It is greed that makes them go to slaughter. A person has power over others. Take people in authority. The power drives them and corruption becomes the need and the greed for more power is the destruction of others. People are either saints or sinners. In this world, most are sinners. Saints do not possess any greed, whether it be money, power or possessions. Do you understand what I'm trying to tell you? It is important for you to temper your needs; your power or you could become one of them. We will work on your controlling your power. You cannot leave here until I am assured of that understanding. Plus there is one other thing that must happen before you can leave. But we will talk about that at another time." Excaliber seemed to tire quickly. His eyelids began to droop and he announced it had been a long day and after such a nice meal he had grown weary.

"One more question, please," asked Isabella.

"Why was it necessary for Salem to teach me the ways of a woman if all I have to do is wish for something?"

Excaliber smiled at Isabella and said, "because you will have to live in a world made up of people that are not one of us and you will need to use their needs against them to get what you want from them. They can be devious and you must learn to stay one step ahead in order to have power over the non-society. Especially men." And with that statement, Excaliber left the room while Isabella sat thinking about her father.

Isabella lay awake most of the night thinking about what all had transpired since she had arrived at the mansion.

She had been told by Electra and Salem that she would be expected to perform sexual favors for Excaliber and yet he had been a perfect gentleman the entire time she had been there. She was bewildered and decided at dinner that night that she would bring up the subject.

Their time so far had been spent learning about one another, although Excaliber had not been as candid as she had been. The reason behind him not making advances toward her had to be because he was her father. That would be incest, and yet she wondered if the sisters were truly her sisters? She had so many questions to ask and never felt confident in prodding him for answers. He had this way about him that always put fear in her asking. However she was determined tonight to at least ask.

The day was spent preparing for the evening dinner. Picking the right attire, making herself as pretty as possible, building her confidence and making a list of the questions she was going to ask. As nervous as she was, she approached the dining room at the dinner hour and found that the table had been set in a most elaborate way with candles and flowers. But Excaliber was not seated at the table.

She took her usual seat and waited. Excaliber was standing in the doorway watching her as she looked over her list of questions. He did not speak and she had no idea how long he had been standing there. He was dressed head to foot in all black and wearing a cape and a fedora. She was somewhat startled by his appearance. He slowly entered the room and seated himself across from her. "That's some outfit," she said, "but aren't you awfully warm?"

He did not remove his hat or cape. Instead remarked, "This is how I shall appear to you from this moment on."

They sat for a few moments in silence and then he left the dining room and again appeared carrying a tray of the potion. She noticed that the glasses were much larger and the foam from the top almost bubbling.

"This is a special potion; much stronger. We are going to have a very special evening tonight," he said. He left the room to retrieve their dinner.

After a quiet dinner with Isabella starting to say things and ask questions, she kept stopping herself trying to judge his mood. He barely looked at her though she knew he was aware that she was watching him. Although the dinner was on par with a gourmet meal, she hardly touched her food. The more silence that prevailed, the more nervous she became.

Finally Excaliber spoke, "Come with me Isabella." He took her hand and led her to a room she had never seen before. When he opened the large French doors, the room caught her breath. It was a large ballroom glowing in dim lights from the many overhead chandeliers and waltz music seemed to come from every direction. As they entered the room, Excaliber took Isabella in his arms and began to waltz about the room. At first the music was slow and dreamy, but it began to get louder and faster and they kept pace with the tempo swirling in sweeping circles about the room. Although Isabella was becoming dizzy, she held on looking into his eyes. He had a blank expression, but gripped her harder and harder.

"The potion is working now and we will do battle," Excaliber shouted. The music suddenly stopped, he released her and she nearly fell to his knees.

All of the questions Isabella intended to ask him left her thinking and she found herself almost to the point of being hypnotized by his glare. As he stood with his piercing look, she thought she might faint when he said, "Stand up straight girl and look at me."

"We have spent this time together, learning to trust and talking of menial things. It is time to get down to the real business of why you are here. Up until now we have played mind games and although you are far advanced you need to know that my powers are far superior to yours. We are done playing games. Go to your room and I will join you momentarily."

Isabella knew not to disobey and ran from the ballroom stopping for just a second to catch her breath at the bottom of the stairs leading up to her room. She stood in the sanctity of her room wishing there was a way to lock on the door. Then the door swung open and there stood Excaliber.

"Follow me," he said. She followed him down a hallway into another room she had also never seen before. The door opened all by itself and they entered.

The room was solid black. The walls, the windows, the furniture were all black. A red glow seemed to fill the room just enough for her to see that this room had to be his bedroom. She could not control the shaking that was taking over her body, and although she wanted to run away, her feet seemed glued to the floor.

He took her shoulders and guided her to the center of the room and then told her to remove her clothing. His voice was deeper than usual. He remained standing and watching her as she slowly began to disrobe. Once she stood in front of him in her nakedness he told her to lie down on the bed. "Now spread your legs. I am taking you now," he announced with such authority and demand that she knew not to argue.

Fully dressed still in cape and fedora he came to the end of the bed. He then removed his hat and cape and got closer. It was then that Isabella noticed the change in his appearance. As he removed his clothing she was astonished by how his physic had changed. He was extremely pale. His body was that of an old man covered in wrinkles and warts. His eyes seemed to glow the red of the room. His soft hands had now become callused and rough. This stranger who was about to place his grotesque body on top of hers frightened her.

With her hands she attempted to push him away. "This is wrong, father," she said. "I can't do this. You are scaring me."

He ignored her plea and the sound of her pleading voice. He took her hand and placed it upon his penis. She was shocked by its size and as it grew harder and harder, bigger and bigger, she knew that it was going to hurt. All of her preparation with Salem did not prepare her for the thrust of his penis inside of her. The tears began to flow from her eyes and her screams seemed muffled even to her. Like she was yelling and yet there was silence.

Once he was done with her, he got off the bed and without saying anything or even looking at her, left the room, shutting the door behind him. She didn't know how long she laid there. She reached down to touch herself and her hand was covered in a combination of blood and his semen. Her thighs ached. Her back ached. Now she began to hear her own sobs.

Somehow Isabella managed to return to her own bedroom. All she wanted to do was shower every inch of her body over and over again. She lay down on her own bed and noticed on the bedside table her list of questions she had memorized to ask that evening. There had been no questions or answers…only rape.

The next morning she began to pack her things. One way or another she was leaving the mansion even if she had to walk. She slipped on a pair of jeans and a shirt, checked to see how much money she had in her wallet and proceeded as quietly as possible down the stairway to the foyer. There in the foyer stood Excaliber in cape and fedora. His appearance had changed back to what she had always seen up until last night. His color was back to normal and his face did not reveal a single wrinkle. How was that possible?

"You are under the impression that you are leaving? That is not going to happen, Isabella. You will not leave this house until I say so. Put your things back into your room and come back down for breakfast," he told her.

"No, I am leaving. How could you treat me like that last night? I hate you. What you did was wrong in so many ways. You are a monster and I am leaving," she screamed. She picked her bag back up and walked toward him as he blocked the front door.

She tried to push passed him but he seemed to grow even taller and wider and with one hand on her arm was able to restrain her from any movement. He knocked the bag from her hand, turned her around and pushed her into the sitting room and onto the sofa.

"I cannot feel compassion for you because of last night. You are doing what is your duty and what you were born to do. The sooner you realize that, the sooner we can get on with it and try to have some sort of a relationship. Quit being such a baby and grow up. Start to realize what opportunity you have and learn to accept it." Excaliber was not going to let her leave and that was his law.

For the next two weeks things were strained between Isabella and Excaliber. Each day was filled with them doing battle mentally. Isabella practiced her "wishing" and causing small disasters around the mansion. She would walk into a room where

Excaliber was seated and make hateful comments, glare at something and cause it to break, or would deliberately shout at him or totally ignore him. He seemed to almost take pride in her antics and would irritate her more by not paying any attention to what she was doing. She refused to eat meals with him and would slip into the kitchen late at night to raid the refrigerator.

One night on a late night run, she opened the refrigerator to find all of the food spoiled. She thought if that was his game, she would beat him at it by wishing for the refrigerator to be filled with delicacies. And the next day it was. She took to wearing the same clothes and not bathing and refused to comb her hair. She walked to the mossy field where the potion plants grew and pulled them all out of the ground. The next day they reappeared healthy and thriving. She tried to enter his bedroom where she planned to destroy it, but that door was always locked and her wishing could not open it. She spent the best time of the day conjuring up terrible things to happen to Excaliber and wishing him dead. Nothing seemed to affect him and yet she could feel herself spiraling into a deep depression. Isabella tried to even read her own tarot to see what the future brought, but every time she picked up her cards, they were blank. She could not find the pouch that held the bones and accused him of stealing them. The only reaction she got was his laugh. She began to think the only way to beat him was to make him think she had decided to join him and so her new plan began.

Each night Excaliber had come to her room and mounted her over this period and although she was disgusted by him, hated him, she had grown more accustomed to his having sex with her. His manner had not changed, his appearance was always of the old man, but she grew more adept in pleasing him in order to get it over with. Now with her new plan she was going to somehow convince him that she was enjoying the ritual and that she was accepting of her position in his society. With his approval perhaps she could flee this prison where she was trapped.

She arrived at the dinner table perfectly dressed and had groomed herself to be the most appealing. She attempted to make polite conversation. His reaction was no reaction. She decided to ask one of the many questions she had thought of approaching all those days before.

"Are the sisters really my sisters," she began? "Are you their father also?"

She poured the potion and handed him his vial. He never even looked up at her. They sat in silence and ate the dinner. She left the dinner table and went upstairs to her room anticipating that he would soon appear at her doorway in his cape and fedora. The hour was growing late and he had not yet come to her room. She decided to go to bed and get a good night's sleep when a tapping at her door suggested otherwise.

When she opened the door, there stood Excaliber dressed in his now usual black but he was holding the Zomba box. Isabella had not seen it since it sat on Electra's lap in the limo that night she had come to the mansion.

"Now that you have gotten all of that hostility out of your system and have tried to show me that you are willing to accept your fate, I have brought you something that will make your life simpler," he said. He placed the box on her bedside table.

Isabella began removing her clothes. "Are we staying here tonight or do we go to your room again," she asked?

"We can stay here, if you would like," and he motioned for her to continue disrobing. When Excaliber had finished with her and began to leave, Isabella asked him, "How long is this going to go on? I have a right to know how long I have to be here with you. Surely you can answer that question?"

"It's a simple answer, Isabella. When you are pregnant with my child, you can return to the other world to give birth. Your sisters will assist you and you will bring the baby to me." His answer was so dry and matter of fact, that Isabella was taken back by the lack of any emotion or sympathy for her. It was obvious now to her that the initiation was to produce a child for him to enslave. Her heartbeat slowed to almost non- existent. How could she possibly win against this monster?

That night after he left, Isabella took Zomba from his box and stared at the floating eyes. They seemed kind and she grew strength in trying to believe that she was not alone in this nightmare. She watched the eyes as they danced about the jar and she interpreted that Zomba was glad to see her again. She whispered to Zomba all her thoughts about Excaliber, how she hated him and what all he does to her. She told him that all of the potion that she had consumed did not seem to have the relaxing way about it anymore, but that on the few days she tried not to drink it, she had horrible headaches and could not seem to function in clear thoughts. Convinced she was now addicted to it, she never missed a dosage. As she continued to pour out her heart to Zomba, she had the distinct feeling that those eyes understood all that she said. And even if Zomba didn't understand, it certainly felt good to confide all her thoughts out loud to a pair of floating eyes.

The days turned into weeks and the weeks into months. Isabella had now lost any idea of exactly how long she had been at the mansion. Each day had begun, slugged on and ended in the exact same manner. The routine of walking the grounds, gathering the moss for potion, sitting on the veranda in the hot sun, dressing for dinner and finishing the night with the old Excaliber inside of her had grown past boredom and melted any and all confidence she might have had once. She took no pride in her appearance. They seldom talked and she knew that until she was pregnant she was a prisoner in Excaliber's mansion. Even their mind games and doing battle over powers had ceased between them. She was beaten and knew it.

Then a strange thing happened. The day started out as usual, but Excaliber never showed at the dining room table. There was no dinner. So after waiting a long period, Isabella fixed herself something to eat and waited in the sitting room. Still no Excaliber. With a surge of energy and a search of the house and surrounding grounds, he was nowhere to be found. Now was her chance to escape. Leaving her belongings in her room, she grabbed her purse and decided to walk out and away from this awful place. It was growing darker and darker, but Isabella was growing stronger and stronger and she began to run down the long driveway believing it would lead to a street.

Hours later, exhausted from running and walking the driveway that never ended, she wondered how this was happening? She knew the driveway was long from the time she had arrived, but it couldn't be this long. She sat down upon the gravel and began to cry. That is when Excaliber suddenly appeared on a black horse, swooped down and picked her up with one motion and placed her behind him on the horse.

Back at the mansion, having not said a word, Excaliber motioned for her to go upstairs. She truly was a prisoner.

That is when she told Excaliber that she was not, nor ever would be pregnant. Her wishing powers of shedding at least one, perhaps two pregnancies in their time together brought on the wrath of Excaliber she had never seen before. He flew into a rage with doors slamming on their own, things breaking and exploding, objects flying through the air directly at her. As she bobbed and ducked to keep from getting hit, she noticed that sometimes the objects boomeranged and flew back at him. As all hell broke loose throughout the house, as his voiced boomed vile pronouncements at her and as she felt her body physically grow in size, the battle continued with the mansion seeming to contract and expand on its own.

Suddenly Excaliber fell to his knees and settled into a fetus position, followed by him appearing to have a seizure by growing, stretching, then back into a fetal position. The sounds coming from him were not human. He was changing to the old man and then back to normal over and over. Shocked and spellbound by what was happening, Isabella found her legs to run to her room and started placing furniture in front of the door.

Everything became very quiet. She stood at the bombarded door and waited knowing that Excaliber would somehow overpower her barricade and is on her once again. That is when she took Zomba out of the box, turned off all of the lights and stood motionless waiting.

The door began to pound. The yelling began to come from outside. She couldn't make out what Excaliber was saying because he seemed to be talking a foreign language punctuated by inhuman sounds. As Isabella stood shaking from head to foot, she began to look for anything that might be a weapon to protect her. Suddenly the furniture moved and in one continuous motion the door flew open and there stood Excaliber his eyes glowing red then changing to green then back to red again. Isabella was terrified. She screamed, "Zomba, please, please help me. Destroy this monster!"

Zomba witnessing what was happening began to grow inside the jar until it exploded. The body of the snake she had only seen once before was in the room between her and Excaliber. Light shafts began to fill the room. Isabella recalled she had seen this happen at Electra's and knew that those shafts would turn into warriors. Hundreds of them filled the room and they descended on Excaliber. Isabella shielded her eyes from the bright lights, but could hear the sound of sucking that grew louder and louder. When the sound subsided, she uncovered her eyes and the shafts of light began to disappear. Zomba stood over the black cape and fedora. Then he turned and gave Isabella a look of dismay. The jar became whole again and Zomba returned to the jar and became just the floating eyes once again.

Cautiously Isabella looked about the house, but Excaliber was not to be found. She then proceeded to where they made the potions and grabbed several large jars and put them in a bag. She then locked the door, retrieved her belongings and began walking the driveway again. This time she did not run, but walked away from the mansion. She wished it to explode. She did not even turn to see if it worked. She could tell by the sound of the explosion that the mansion was gone.

She looked up into the dawning sky and announced to the heavens, "I am free."

The Sinners of New Orleans

The Story of Isabella Amadour Smithers

Part Two

Chapter ONE

A New Life

The **Red Garter** was gearing up for Mardi Gras. The steady dinner crowd was now surpassed by the lunch crowd. Isabella hated Mardi Gras. Opening the **Red Garter** for the tourists who couldn't afford to eat dinner, but were standing in line at 11:00 a.m. to partake of the smaller portions at the cheaper prices, was not her idea.

Jazz was standing at the reception desk when Baker Epson entered and wound his way through the standing groups of hungry customers waiting to be seated for lunch. He couldn't help but notice that Jazz was very tall and slender with bright green eyes the likes he had never seen. Her long brown hair was pulled to one side and he greeted her with his best smile and handed her his card.

It read "Baker Epson, Inspector."

"I'm here to inspect the kitchen. Will you please tell Ms. Smithers that I'm here?"

Jazz called out the name "Wilson, party of six," and then turned her attention to Mr. Epson and asked him to step to one side. "I believe Isabella is here; let me call the office," she said.

Jazz then picked up the house phone and called back to Isabella's office. The phone rang several times before Isabella answered with a tart reply, "Yes, what is it?"

Jazz explained that an inspector was in the lobby and wanted to see her and inspect the kitchen. "I'll be right out. Tell him to go to the bar."

"You picked a hell of a time to come, Baker. Couldn't this wait?"

"I'm sorry Isabella, but you know we don't announce and what better time to see that you are up to par than when you are so busy?" Baker Epson could hardly control his excitement at seeing Isabella again. He was fascinated by her and admired what she had accomplished at the **Red Garter** in the time she had taken over what was now New Orleans' most famous restaurant. He was once again taken with her beauty and her demeanor. She asked him if he would like a drink, which he declined, and followed her back to her office.

The office now had a more feminine feel to it with big over-stuffed lounge chairs, soft lighting and the aroma of perfume. The desk that Bill

Smithers had sat at for years still remained.

"Hard to believe it has been almost a year, Baker, since the last inspection. And it seems strange to see you in this capacity since I haven't seen you in the *Back Door* for quite a while. Did you give up gambling?"

Baker Epson lowered his head and then replied, "The wife told me she'd leave me and take the kids if I didn't stop. So I turned in my key."

"Sorry to hear that, especially with a great gathering of New Orleans finest about to participate in the *Big Bet* coming up. We will miss you. But if you change your mind, just let me know and I'll forego the key," Isabella stated nonchalantly. "Now let's see what's going on in the kitchen. Bring your little pad and let's get on with it. I'm a very busy woman!"

Baker Epson half-heartily did his job always glancing toward Isabella as she spoke to the chefs and waiters in the hurry scurry of the kitchen. The special today was Redfish Courtbouillon and Duck a la Patout at a third of the cost to the patrons.

"I'll be in my office when you have finished. You can bring the certificate signed Baker Epson, as I am sure you will." She gave him her most determined eye and left the kitchen.

Back in the office, Isabella poured herself a drink, sat down in the chaise lounge in the corner and began fingering the picture of Bill sitting next to her in a silver frame.

It was still hard for her to accept he was gone. She missed him desperately, but being in the Red Garter every day made him feel close to her. Bill and the Red Garter had been her salvation. The tap at the door and Baker's voice brought her back to the moment.

"Come in, Baker," she replied. Isabella was now standing behind the desk as Baker handed her the new certificate. "No problems I assume," she asked?

"Of course not, Isabella. But I would clean that overhead fan soon," he said. "Say when is the *Big Bet*?"

"Oh, are you considering buying in? We have a full house, but we could find you some room I'm sure. But you have to let me know immediately. It's $5000.00 this year. I'll tell Culotta to expect you if you got the cash. It's this Friday at 1:00 a.m."

"Will Jazz at the reception desk be there?" he asked.

"Yes, she'll be there. She is one of my most popular girls. Interested, huh?"

Baker Epson left Isabella's office, made his way through the dining room toward the front lobby and stopped to say goodbye to Jazz. She ignored him.

Isabella then rang the reception desk and asked Jazz to find Culotta and send him to her office. She then poured herself another short one, sat back down in the chaise and began looking over the list of prominent names that had registered to play in the *Big Bet*. She couldn't help but grin to herself at the list of judges, bankers, industry captains and politicians who had easily and quickly forked over their five grand for entry into the *Back Door*. The *Big Bet* was a big deal and a lot of money would be circulating that night along with New Orleans' most desired courtesans. Jazz had already been promised to Judge Persell.

"Isabella, its Culotta," the retired police officer and now Isabella's personal body guard at her office door.

"Come in, take a seat, Frank. We need to talk about Friday. You are going to need some extra help and I want fellas you can depend on for their complete discretion. We are expecting the largest and most conspicuous crowd we have ever had at the *Back Door*. Absolutely no cameras. I want someone at the head of the alley, in the alley, at the brick wall at the end of the alley, two men at the door. Everyone must show their key. All except Baker Epson. He turned his in some time ago, but may be joining us. I'll let you know about that. No one is to be admitted before 1:00 a.m. No one! Everyone on foot. No limos or cars can enter the alley, understood? I want six men in the room circulating. I have two security wands to use at the door. Everyone is to be checked, but with dignity and good manners. If you should encounter anyone with a weapon, confiscate it, bring it to my office where it will be locked in the vault and returned when they leave. The girls will already be at the *Back Door* lobby waiting. I'll be checking them and giving them instructions. Your men must keep their hands to themselves. To them the girls are just eye candy. Nothing more. Is that understood? Now, Frank, you've been with me a very long time and I know I can count on you to follow my instructions to the letter. Don't let me down. Can you get that many men you can trust?"

"Will you be joining us at all that evening?" Culotta inquired.

"Oh I will make an appearance once I know New Orleans' greatest have all arrived, but I do not intend to stay. I'll be spending the night in the office. I want the names and numbers, addresses of each and every man on duty that night. Inform them that if any of my rules are broken there will be hell to pay and they'll never see New Orleans again. Stress that in only the way you can, my dear."

Frank almost bowed. "I'll have that list for you by tonight. I've got a good idea of who I'll call. All of them can be depended upon, I assure you." Frank took a few steps backward, turned and left the office closing the door quietly.

Frank Culotta had retired from the police force and was working as a night watchman at one of the freight docks on the Mississippi when one day a beautiful woman had approached him in Tujague's while having a beer on a late winter's day. She looked familiar, but he couldn't place her. Then she spoke.

"Aren't you Officer Culotta," she asked? I'm Isabella Amadour. Do you remember me?"

Frank stared at her and then suddenly he recalled the young girl he had met after her mother had been run down on Canal Street by a hit and run driver. He had gone to the funeral. It all came rushing back to him. But so much time had passed. The young girl was now a grown woman and was even more beautiful than he had remembered.

"Yes, I do remember who you are. How have you been? I have not seen you in the Quarter in several years. You are all grown up now. Do you still live here?" I went back to the Pearl and even stopped by you and your mother's apartment, but no one knew where you had gone. It's been a long time."

"A lot has happened in that time. Did you ever find out who killed Marta?" Isabella knew the answer to that question, but wanted to know if the officer had ever been able to piece together any suspicions. "I couldn't stay in that apartment and I found some people who took me in and I learned a craft and made the best of my life as I could. It was hard. I've been through a lot, but I'm fine now and quite happy."

"That crime remained unsolved and after a while in *this* city it was abandoned from any further investigation. I'm retired now and working as a night watchman. It's boring as hell, but it pays for the extras. Cops don't make much pension, ya know," the officer responded.

Isabella sat down on the stool next to him and ordered a beer. They sat there for well over an hour making small talk and laughing at some of his stories about being on the force. Frank Culotta was enjoying talking to this pretty woman and couldn't help but notice everyone noticing them. He sat a little straighter on the stool. She announced she had to get back to work, but enjoyed talking with him. He asked where she was working and he noticed she sat up straighter on her stool when she said, "I'm the hostess at the **Red Garter**. You know the restaurant?"

"Everyone knows that place, Isabella. Never eaten there. Can't afford it, but I know it is popular and suppose to be the best in the city."

"Tell you what, Frank…may I call you Frank….come by sometime and your dinner is on me. I'll see to it you got the best table in the joint. But you got to wear a jacket and tie or they will escort you out the door," she said with a pat on his back and a giggle. She paid for all the beers and walked out the door of Tujague's into the cold wind.

It took some courage and some time passing before Frank Culotta ever showed up at the **Red Garter**. He was wearing a new navy blue suit, new shoes that pinched his feet and a clean white shirt with a bolo tie. He had admired himself in the mirror after making several shirt changes and decided this was a good day for a good meal.

Isabella hardly recognized her policeman friend when he entered the lobby. But as soon as she did, she burst into her biggest smile. "I'm so glad to see you, Frank. I hope you are hungry? I want you to meet someone. Stay right there." Isabella left the lobby and returned with a handsome man who Isabella introduced as William Smithers, the owner of the **Red Garter** and her fiancée.

After the dinner that Frank said was the best meal he had ever eaten, Bill and Isabella joined him in after dinner drinks. The three of them became very good friends after that night. And William Smithers offered him a job as a security/bouncer at the **Red Garter** at four times the money he was making as a watchman. Frank became a fixture in the bar and at the front door almost 10 years ago.

Part Two

Chapter TWO

The Big Bet

Isabella was now living on St. Charles Street with a staff of three: a maid, a cook and an assistant to help her in all of her business affairs. She had informed all of them that she would be staying at her office that night. It was Friday; the night of the *Big Bet* and she wouldn't be home until late the next morning.

St. Charles was littered with beads hanging from the trees and street lamps as parade after parade had made its way down the fabled street. She was glad that it was over and that most of the party crowds had dwindled to the usual tourists and the trash was half the amount in the Quarter. The natives of the city could get back to regular lives and the **Red Garter** was now only opened for dinner. But she still had to get through this one last night of quiet chaos at the *Back Door*.

While her maid helped her pack a bag and pick out the outfit she was going to wear making her entrance into the *Back Door* for the *Big Bet*, she had wished she had followed her instincts to discontinue the *Back Door* after the first of the year. But it was too late now and when she calculated the amount of money it provided and the service to the "book" she was keeping on all of her associates that participated, it seemed not to her advantage to shut it down. Over the years she had been able to keep records on the city's most valued citizens that had always given her the upper hand in dealing with them. Bill had taught her well. Because of him she had learned to observe and keep a record on these dignitaries and whenever any kind of a problem arose, she knew who to speak to and get results. Or else. They never called it blackmail. They called it "keeping book." And it always worked.

Bill always lived by the statement, "Keep your friends close and your enemies closer!"

In order to have access to the *Back Door*, a large room filled with crap tables, blackjack tables and poker tables only, you had to purchase a key. That key opened a door on the back alley behind the building next door to the **Red Garter**. It was the only way in and out known to the key holders. Only Bill, Isabella and Frank knew of the special entrance from the **Red Garter** kitchen to the closet of the *Back Door*.

The *Back Door* had no windows. The room was painted dark grey and furnished with a full bar the length of one wall. There was a Ladies and Men's room, a coat checkroom and a small lounge behind a curtain just to the left of the entrance. A guard stood at that curtain at all times. And he stood next to the guard at the front door.

No food was provided at the *Back Door*. However the liquor was plentiful. It usually took three bartenders to handle the orders. Many a time the key holders offered huge tips to the women who worked the *Back Door* to be their drink runners. And if a key holder desired more from his runner than a drink, he could offer her the lounge behind the curtain at a hefty cost plus tip. The guard would see that no one disturbed them. Only the most desirable women were employed at the *Back Door*. All of them had to have regular jobs, a college education, be in the best shape physically and mentally and were not permitted to drink while on the premises. Their dress code was very upscale. If someone showed up provocatively dressed, she was sent home. Hair had to be styled neatly, nails had to be manicured with no polish and only minimum amount of jewelry was permitted.

These women knew they would be catering to the city's elite and that the connections they would make could change their lives. And the money was outstanding. Only Isabella had the say as to who could work the *Back Door*.

The women generally were observed working at the **Red Garter** and approached after a year's service as to whether they would be interested in working the *Back Door*. Not every lovely lady accepted the offer, however those that did knew a good thing and would never do anything to deprive themselves of the opportunity to make such large paychecks and network in such a way that would change their lives forever. Isabella never considered she was running a brothel. There were plenty of those in New Orleans. No women working the *Back Door* had to succumb to sex unless it was her choice.

The men who purchased the key to the *Back Door* knew all the rules. Every year your key was changed to match the changing lock. The cost was $10,000.00 per year. With that fee paid you were guaranteed anonymous entry, guaranteed protection from the law and always a good time. On special events like the *Big Bet* there was an additional fee and free booze. The discretion of each key holder was paramount to protect the whole. Whenever a key holder talked too much, did not behave in a gentlemanly fashion, could not pay his debts or created any kind of scandal in the city, his key was revoked and he was banned from every social function in the city. Thus was the power of the *Back Door*. The only way you could even be considered to be a part of this elite men's club was to have your name submitted to Isabella who would then proceed to do such an intense back ground check with her many sources and then you would be on probation. If any member key holder found reason to state a complaint, you were black balled for life.

Isabella understood the need for men to have a place where they could be free to be boys, where they could do their boasting, shoot off their mouths, exhibit their egos and compare their dicks in the form of power and money. All of this while showing off in front of beautiful women. They also understood that the beautiful women could say no with no repercussions. Otherwise one of the brute security guards escorted you home.

And so after many years of the *Back Door*, the *Big Bet* and the beautiful women, Isabella felt as though she provided a service to the influential men of New Orleans....and a good place to eat.

Isabella also understood that she benefited greatly by providing this service. Her mansion on St. Charles St. was paid in full by the keys and fees of the *Back Door*. The connections she made within the city fathers benefited her greatly also. Whenever there was a problem, it was solved with a phone call.

As Isabella entered her office at the **Red Garter**, the telephone was ringing. It was the outside line. Debating whether to answer it, she heard the answer machine pick up and it was Baker Epson's voice informing her that he would not be there for the *Big Bet*. She then called Frank Culotta and informed him not to look for Baker Epson.

She unpacked her bag, hung up the black velvet skirt and jacket, the solid gold blouse and her dark stockings in preparation for changing later. She picked up the final list of event comers that night and stood at the window of her office perusing it with flashbacks of names and events that had brought her to this moment.

The name Charles James DuCote was at the top. She closed her eyes to recall his face. He had become a new key member only the year before based on his rising status as the new bank vice president and a friend of the mayor. The mayor was also expected that night. "The movers and the shakers," Isabella thought.

She called down to the bar to ask if Jazz was in yet. When Creaky answered the phone he told her he had not seen her yet that day, but when he did he would tell her to report. Jazz was the mayor's favorite and she wondered whether arrangements had been made?

The rest of the women would be arriving somewhere around midnight. Until then Isabella had plenty of paper work to attend to. The restaurant would be closed to the general public that night and only opened to key holders for a good meal before the gambling began. Not many had signed up for dinner. They were probably all sneaking out of their homes on feeble excuses to show up at 1:00 a.m. There was the menu to inspect, the liquor list for the *Back Door* and a nap after a late lunch would be necessary. Isabella made herself comfortable for a long day and night.

At 11:00 p.m. Isabella began with a shower in her office bath, and then started doing her hair and makeup. She still performed the expert application as Salem had taught her. Her mind wandered back to Salem's face and the friendship they had shared. That was so long ago, but she thought of Salem often. Isabella had tried to find Salem at one time, but it was though she never existed.

Isabella looked at herself in the full mirror and decided that Salem would have thought she looked beautiful. Perhaps even more beautiful now. Passing her own inspection of the overall look and deciding she approved, she then did something she had not done in a very long time. She unlocked a cupboard door, took a swig of the potion and lifted the drape over Zomba's jar. The eyes were closed.

Isabella was disappointed in the fact she seemed not to control her mind from going back to a place she wanted to forget. It was like a voice inside her head beckoning her to remember and although she tried to put it all out of her mind, it simply would not stop haunting her that day. "Why today am I dwelling on such things?' she asked herself. She was grateful for the interruption of the office phone telling her the women had arrived and were waiting at the bar. The dining room only had a half dozen key holders that were finishing their meals and smoking cigars.

Isabella approached the 10 women at the bar, told Creaky to see to it that the cigar smoke dissipates when the last man leaves and turned her attention to the ladies.

"Well ladies are you ready for this evening?" Isabella was checking out their appearances from head to foot as she spoke.

Jazz spoke up first. "Sorry Isabella, I just arrived. Did you want to see me special?"

"No, I just wanted you to know you were spoken for tonight. You'll be with Judge Persell, that's all."

"I sort of figured as much," she replied. One of the girls let out a whoop that was met and stifled immediately by a glare from Isabella.

"Ok ladies, you know what to do. You all look gorgeous. Now act as beautiful as you look."

The ladies left the bar, headed out the door and walked around the corner to the alley where they were greeted by the security guard who could not help but smile at all of them. He knew he would never have the pleasure of their company, but he certainly could look at them. Few of them spoke as their high heels sounded on the pavement and broken stones as they approached the door. Culotta greeted them each by name.

At 1:00 a.m. the first of the key holders began to arrive. They were saluted by the small group that had just come around the corner from the restaurant. There was a lot of backslapping and hand shaking as they strolled down the alley.

The night was going to be a lot of politicking and promises, most of which were not to be kept or even remembered by dawn. Their pockets were bulging with fat wallets of money and all were in hopes of being the biggest winner. But the boasting would remain behind those closed doors.

Everyone was in place and the night began slightly subdued, but soon changed to loud talk and bursts of laughter.

Isabella made her entrance around 2:00 a.m. She rounded each table speaking to each individual by asking about their children and grandchildren. She knew many of them from being introduced in the **Red Garter**. She spoke to Charles James DuCote and asked about his daughter Lyn. "She must be almost grown by now Charles," she asked? And Mayor how is that new house you are building in Plaquemine Parish coming along? I understand it is costing the tax payers a real pretty penny!"

"Oh now Missy Isabella, you know better than that. That house is being built with my investments. And what I plan to leave here with tonight," he heartily laughed.

"Don't be too sure of that Mayor. I see who is at your table. Why do you think the police chief and the publisher of the Picayune, not to mention our congressman here, will let you get out of the door with a penny in your pocket! I think you are doomed kind sir if they have anything to do with it." Isabella flashed him a big smile, pecked his check with a soft kiss and moved on to the next table to greet the C.E.O.s and the bankers. One was holding a full house and she winked at him from the next table.

Along about 3:00 Isabella excused herself as the men were getting louder and more relaxed. The betting had reached an all-time high and the booze was beginning to take its toll in their judgement. As she opened the door to the closet a roar came up from the craps table where the owner of most of the slum housing in New Orleans was scoring big rolling his number. The last thing she heard was, "let it ride!"

In the solitude of her office, Isabella kicked off her high heels, poured herself a drink and fell into the big soft easy chair next to the desk. She reached over and put her favorite tape in the player, closed her eyes and drifted in and out of a fitful sleep.

With a sudden start she awoke thinking she heard voices in the room. She noticed that tears were wet on her cheeks and she shook her head awake completely trying to recall what she may have been dreaming. Then in a rush she knew she was dreaming about Bill. Nights like tonight she missed him the most.

She switched on the reading lamp at the desk, unlocked the bottom desk drawer and pulled out the scrapbook she kept hidden. The burgundy red leather was worn and the binding was given way to many hours of looking at the newspaper clippings and pictures she now once again stared at with sadness.

There was the happiest day in her life. The bride and groom so in love. She had put on a few pounds and had begun to color her hair, but essentially she still looked the same. The white suit and petite veil she was wearing was still in a box in her closet at home. The announcement in the paper of Mr. and Mrs. William Smithers will celebrate their wedding in Italy and will spend the next month honeymooning throughout Europe was the lead story on the Society page of the Times Picayune. It only took Bill Smithers wooing Isabella two years before she finally said yes. She had been so hesitant and afraid that Bill would find out who she was, what she had done and that he would not understand her past. She never told him everything, but enough so that he accepted her as not only non- virginal, but someone with a black background that could hurt his reputation.

She had shown up at the **Red Garter** after hours and pounded on the door. He peered through the glass and saw it was Isabella and instantly opened the door and took her into his arms. They sat up all night talking, with her trying to explain where she had been for such a long time without telling him all of the truth. She never mentioned Excaliber or Electra, but led him to believe that after her mother's death she was lost and a group of people that she referred to as a cult had taken her in and befriended her.

She glanced sideways at him to see if there was to be a reaction to that particular comment. She still didn't know who had approached him so long ago to tell him she could not work the part-time job he had offered her. With no interruption, she continued to say she had run away and he was the only one she thought to flee to.

He just seemed very happy to see her again.

Shortly after that she began working as the hostess at the **Red Garter**. Two years later they were married and she had never been happier. They made a good team in the restaurant. She caught on quickly and soon her confidence in being a regular human being with a man in her life that loved her, a good job and a future became normal.

She was very good at avoiding any subject that she found objectionable or hurtful to them. She focused on being a good wife, a good employee and later a partner in the **Red Garter**. He understood that they would never have children and that never seemed to bother him. He was a contented man.

Isabella turned the page a couple of times in the scrapbook and then stopped and looked at the newspaper clipping about the big mansion out in the bayous that had suddenly exploded and burned to the ground. As she read the clipping, a smile that turned into a deep throaty laugh broke the silence in the room. She recalled walking that path away from the mansion, hearing the explosion and yelling "Go To Hell" at the top of her lungs.

Thinking about the past caused her much sorrow. Isabella could not recount how much time had gone by from the moment she fled the mansion,

Excaliber, the society and such and had made her way back into a real world. It was as though the explosion of the mansion had caused her mind to fragment into as many pieces as the mortar, brick and stone. She would get glimpses of what had happened in sweaty dreams and flashes of sights in the daylight. It was hard for her to put all the pieces together into one continuous thought. She could not recall in detail how she had gotten back to the city. She remembered wandering in the bayou searching for anything familiar. Strangers she encountered were unknown to her and somehow she managed to forage for food, stole clothes from a cabin wash line and bathed herself in brackish waters. But how much time had passed was a mystery to her. Her only possession was the bag of jars containing the potion.

Part Two

Chapter THREE

The Knock at the Door

The *Big Bet* was in full swing. Isabella had made her entrance with all the charm she could muster, the girls were busy entertaining and serving the guests' needs and she was content to sit and reminisce in the quiet office. The knock at her office door brought her back to the moment of present time. She glanced at the clock which read almost 4:30 a.m. and wondered who would have the nerve to disturb her at this hour...unless there was a problem.

"Yes, who is it? she answered.

"It's Frank, Isabella. May I come in?"

Frank entered Isabella's office and apologized for disturbing her, but stated quickly that there was a problem that only she could address. He went on to explain that the Governor had arrived about an hour ago without his key and had insisted on coming in. He was not on the list, but Frank didn't want to disturb her and thought it would be okay if he paid his entry. Frank had accepted his money in cash and found him a seat at the table with Bishop Perch figuring the Bishop would keep him in check.

"I was wrong, Isabella, and now he is causing trouble. When I asked him to leave, he became very loud and foul. At first everyone tried to ignore him and that only made him angry and he socked the Bishop's jaw when the Bishop told him he wasn't welcome among upstanding members and should leave without acting the fool. Well, that did it and the Gov. hit him." Frank apologized again and mumbled he probably should have not let him come the first place.

"Where is he now? And where is the Bishop?" Isabella was now angry herself. At all of them, including Frank.

"The Bishop is being attended to by two of the girls and the Governor is still in the alley with two of the security guys. What do you want me to do?"

"Bring the Governor around to the front entrance of the restaurant and I'll meet you there as soon as I see to the Bishop. Frank, you know the history and should have known better than to make that decision to let him in. No key, no entrance in spite of cash!"

Isabella slipped on a silk robe and her high heel slippers and entered the *Back Door* as quietly as possible ignoring anyone that looked her way. She approached the lounge area behind the curtain and found Jazz, Pris and Delilah attending to the Bishop who appeared to be quite content even with a swollen jaw and a bruise forming.

"David, are you alright?" she inquired.

"That rat bastard hit me," he reported. "Once a lying politician, always a lying prick. He'd cheat his own grandmother. And he's a drunk. What was he doing here?" It was obvious to Isabella that the bad blood between them would last their lifetimes.

"I am very sorry. Frank made a dreadful mistake letting him in and I will reprimand him for it, I assure you. As for the Governor, you let me take care of him. I will fix it that you will never need to encounter him again in this or any of my establishments. Was he drunk? Oh, never mind. It's not important, but what is important is, are you alright?"

Pris was holding and caressing his hand, while Jazz was pouring him another shot of whiskey. Delilah was applying a cold cloth to his jaw trying to reduce the swelling. He smiled at Delilah and told Isabella that the girls were easing the pain.

Isabella slipped out of the lounge, returned to the closet entrance and proceeded to the front door of the **Red Garter**. There in the last rays of gas lit streetlights she could make out the figures of the Governor and the two security guards still holding him on each side. She unlocked the door and the three entered the dark restaurant. She motioned for the guards to place him on the lobby bench and then told them to remain right outside.

"Sir, you have caused me grief tonight. Frank made a serious error permitting your entrance and it will cost him, but as for you Governor, your grief has just begun. I have tolerated you for years. This city has put up with your corruption and behavior and any favors anyone has ever done for you was in that room. This is the last. Wasn't it enough that that Bible- beating, wet-behind- the-ears kid beat the socks off of you in your last election? Your wife left you. Your kids don't speak to you. You're nothing but a drunk and you have provoked the two people in this world that can make you disappear. You are a stupid man, Governor and I'm through."

He sat slumped on the bench looking in Isabella's direction, but appeared to be staring at the picture of Bill Smithers behind her on the wall. It was barely visible in the dim light, but the Governor focused on the picture.

"Bill would have understood, Isabella. It's been hard," the Governor whispered.

"Governor, you made all your own heartache. No one is to blame, but you. I don't give a damn anymore about your troubles. Bill, me, even David tried to help you out of that jam. We kept our mouths shut and did what we could, but you destroyed your life, not us. And the thanks we get are more trouble. You would do yourself and this city a big favor if you left and never came back. If you don't, I am afraid others will see to it that you simply disappear altogether. Do you understand? Are you listening to me?" Isabella was losing her patience with a man who was once respected and most powerful, but now was a mere degenerate.

"Do you ever hear from Sharon?" he questioned.

"That does it. I'm done with you. My men will drive you home. I suggest you pack up today and head out. I won't be responsible for what happens to you. As for Sharon, that is no longer any of your business. You should never even mention her name if you know what's good for you."

Isabella opened the front door, said a few whispered words to the security guards who then took the Governor by both shoulders and escorted him to a waiting car.

Isabella closed and locked the door, turned and walked back toward her office. Daylight was slightly appearing through the office window when she called Frank back to her office via a walkie talkie.

A few minutes later a weak knock at the door and Frank's voice could barely be heard. He opened the door sheepishly and took a few steps forward.

"Sit down Frank. We need to get something straight. Anything I say to you now is in the strictest confidence and if you ever open your mouth, you'll suffer more than just being fired. Is that understood?"

Frank could tell from her expression and the anger in her voice that he had better listen closely and not interrupt. He took a chair across from the desk she was now sitting at and waited for his fate.

Isabella poured herself a glass of orange juice and handed Frank a bottle of champagne to open for a mimosa. After inquiring if he wanted one and his head shaking no, she motioned for him to pour the champagne and began:

"Years ago when Bill and I were very happy running the **Red Garter** and business was good, I did not think my life would be so full of joy. We loved running the restaurant together. We had just moved into the house on Camp Street and spent as much time as possible renovating it when we were not here. I enjoyed meeting and greeting all of the movers and shakers of the city when they came for dinner. Some of them actually became friends and we occasionally socialized at a party or had them to our home. Bill was so respected, but I thought it was for the same reasons I did. He was genuinely a nice guy and did folks a lot of favors. But as we grew closer and he had confidence in me as a true partner, he would confide in me about certain individuals. At first I was sort of shocked at what he told me, but then after a while nothing shocked me. Growing up in the city, I always knew there were a lot of deals made, and a lot of shady things going on. The papers sometimes reported a scandal that I had known about from Bill months before any reporter ever got wind. My background was not at all what they would have thought respectable, so we always told them that we had met and then I left the city for awhile and when I came back we started dating and fell in love. But few people, other than you, knew about Marta or what was in my past and we kept it that way. Funny. If they had known, most of them would have accepted me anyway, but it was better left untold. The city was changing and the Governor was a big part of that change.

He was a young pup then on the rise in the Republican Party. He was full of ideas to fix the city and a lot of people listened. The idiots! They actually thought he could clean up New Orleans! But like every cop or politician on the rise with the best intentions, they all become greedy and think they are above the law. In this city, it's the only way. You know that. Promises are made, money…big money…starts to cross palms and the next thing you know you become more corrupt than the next guy. All the while pretending to be what the people want. What fools!

It did not take long for the Governor to get a Representative seat, then a senate and begin thinking about being the Governor. He was happily married, with a couple of kids, a devout Catholic always photographed leaving St. Mary's on Sunday, but never photographed leaving the *Back Door*. Hell, I didn't even question Bill about the *Back Door* for over a year because secretly I did not want to know what went on there. I knew it involved gambling and that's all I wanted to know.

Then one night Bill came home very late and said there had been some trouble. He told me that the Governor had gotten one of the girls pregnant and that he had been asked to take care of it, you know make the arrangements. That did not surprise me, but what followed caused a lot of people a lot of problems. I had met Sharon, she was one of our best waitresses and she was asked to help serve at the *Back Door*. She met the newly elected Governor and was not only smitten, but as it turned out a real gold digger. They had been seeing one another for a while and Bill had made it possible. The Governor knew he could count on Bill's discretion, but when Bill found out what the Governor had done, it caused a big rift between them which spread to Bishop David Perch and me.

Long story short, Sharon refused to get rid of the baby but instead threatened to make it publicly known in order for his wife to leave him and marry her. I suspect his wife knew he was cheating on her from the rumors that flew through the Quarter, but she wasn't about to make it easy on him. Because of all the anxiety that the Governor's wife was causing, he had a doctor friend suggest a pill known as thalidomide prescribed for her. It must have worked because she stopped causing problems for him at home. But with Sharon pushing and demanding things, the Governor slipped her one in a drink while at the *Back Door*.

Sharon did calm down, but every time she acted up again, the Governor would mickey her drink again. When Bill had neglected to convince Sharon to get rid of the baby, he instead asked me to take her up north to a clinic that performed abortions behind closed doors. When she saw where she was being taken, she ran away and I could not find her. I searched everywhere; I even called the police. But she just disappeared. When I informed Bill, he told me to come on home that he would deal with it from that point. I worried about her for months. I would ask Bill if the Governor heard from her and he always said there had been no word.

Then one day, I got a call at the restaurant and it was Sharon. She had gone into labor, was out of money and was in some hospital in West Virginia. She begged me to come. She did not have anyone else to call.

I was there when the baby was born. It was so deformed. It had no feet and stubbed arms. I don't think with those eyes it could see. I passed myself off as her sister and the doctors kept asking me what they should do. Seeing that baby made me sick.

The doctors handled Sharon by telling her the baby had died. She did not cry. She only asked when she could leave. The baby was alive, but we all agreed that something had to be done with the child. I called Bill and explained everything.

Bill flew with a pilot on a private plane out of Lakefront and I met him at a small private runway outside of Elkins, West Virginia. He put me on that plane and sent me home assuring me he would take care of everything. All I wanted to do was go home.

It took him two days to return home. He simply walked in the restaurant and said not to worry, all was taken care of and he didn't wish to speak of it again. It was a few years later that I found out what happened. I heard from Sharon only a couple of times after that. She was living in New York City, but questioned whether the Governor ever asked about her. I told her no. But of course he did. Neither one of them ever asked about the baby...ever. And that bastard never paid Bill back for all of his expenses. Bill told me that someday he would call his favor in and that it did not concern me anymore."

Frank was listening intently, but finally asked, "but you know what happened to the baby?"

Isabella hesitated, took a deep breath and told Frank they had sold the baby to a shoddy traveling freak show.

Both of them sat in silence for a long minute.

"I thought the whole incident over with and never gave it any more thought, until one day a lady came into the lobby of the restaurant. She looked familiar, but I could not place her. When she stepped into the light and pulled her hood back away from her face, I knew in an instant who she was. She was someone from my past that I thought must be dead. She was very old and crippled, but I recognized those eyes. Her name was Electra and she had befriended me after my mother had died. She stared at me, her eyes narrowing and finally she spoke in a gravel voice, "I have the baby."

Well, I was totally taken back, but did not lose my composure. I merely asked, "What baby?"

"What happened next," Frank asked?

"I'm exhausted Frank. That's enough. Perhaps someday, if I'm in another reminiscent mood, I'll tell you more. But for now, keep your mouth shut, do you understand? You're dismissed. Go home."

Part Two

Chapter FOUR

Isabella and Creaky

Isabella had always led people to believe that Creaky was her nephew Gerald. It was just simpler that way, when in fact Isabella had never met Creaky before those long ago days when she first met Bill and had gone to the **Red Garter** for a cup of coffee and discussion about a part-time job. Their first meeting may have been brief, but it altered both of their lives.

Discussion with Frank Culotta had opened wounds that Isabella felt were necessary to heal. The only way she could do that was to face facts, forgive others and especially herself. She studied her face in the mirror and thought to herself that she simply had to somehow force herself to remember everything.

She then did something she promised herself she would never do again.

Isabella gathered the tarot cards, the bones, the empty jars of potion, all the reminders of the past. She placed them in front of her and with her hands passing over each object, she willed the face staring back at her in the mirror to go deep into a trance. Then suddenly the room became dark and filled with mist. She thought she heard a voice calling to her and just as she was about to become the past and present in the mirror, she arose and went to the cabinet and pulled out the box containing the jar of Zomba's floating eyes. They were wide open watching her and it startled her because they had been closed for years.

She placed Zomba in the middle of the vanity and put both hands on either side of the jar. She then stared at the mirror once again. The room darkened. The mist began to thicken and swirl. Isabella's heart was pounding as though it would burst out of her breast.

"I need to know. I need to remember. I need to see my crimes. I implore you to show me my life as it was, so that I can begin to heal."

Isabella's eyes looked deep into the mirror. Her face was the only true reflection, but Isabella did not see her face. Instead she saw images of the past. At first they were all jumbled up with pictures of people fading in and out while her conscious mind tried to focus on each. It was all happening so fast that it became impossible. There was Sasha, then Salem, then Bill, then Excaliber. They swirled so quickly that it appeared to be one's eyes, another's mouth and yet another's smile.

Isabella could feel heat coming from the jar containing Zomba emitting into her hands. She continued to clutch the jar and watch the mirror as the figures began to take more true form and present themselves in better focus.

There was Isabella sitting on the front stoop entrance to the apartment she loved on Esplanade, but she recognized the fact that it wasn't in the happier time of moving into it….no she was older, dressed in stolen clothes and then realized this had to be upon her arrival back in the city after the mansion and Excaliber. Someone was approaching her, but it was hard to make out who it was. Then she saw that it was a man and he was handing her something in a large envelope. When she bent her face down to see what was in the envelope and saw that it was thousands of dollars in a bundle and looked up, he was gone.

The next image changed to this same unrecognized man escorting her to the field behind the burned out mansion and they were gathering the mossy fungus that was the potion. She strained to see was it Excaliber? No, it was that man with the envelope, but who was he? They then began to mix the potion in a basement she could not see clearly enough to place in her mind.

The images were all getting confusing again, so she implored Zomba to help her continue to see her life as it was. There was Salem making love to her who instantly became Excaliber on top of her. Electra's voice was heard speaking of initiation and then Marta appeared in the mirror and the smell of *Evening in Paris* perfume filled the room.

Isabella had no concept of present time passing and was sitting in a pool of sweat while beads formed all over her body. She was suddenly brought back out of the mirror by the ringing sound of the telephone in the room. Like a ghost evaporating before her eyes she was thrust back to reality in a shaken state.

She slowly rose from the chair in front of the mirror and in a wobble moved toward the ringing telephone and yanked it out of the wall and tossed it across the room. She then entered the hallway and hollered down the stairs to any of her house employees within ear shot that she was "not to be disturbed under any, and I mean any, circumstances!"

She returned to her bedroom and tried to decide whether she was in any condition to continue this journey. Fortified by the need to know, the confidence that she could put herself back into the trance, she sat back down and began again. Only this time was harder and different. The images were quick to return, but she did not want to continue. There was Marta dead in her casket replaced by her beloved Bill. She tried to pull herself away, but could not. She was weeping as the remains of Bill were placed in the mausoleum and she stared in disbelief as the attendant sealed the tomb.

She saw images of hell with the shards of light that had consumed Excaliber. She saw Zomba's eyes laughing. It was too much and she forced herself to pull back away from the mirror.

Crying hysterically and shaking from head to foot, Isabella collapsed onto the floor.

How long she lied there she could not determine for the clock's hands had not moved.   When she became fully conscious once again, she felt very strange and different. Instead of feeling lighter and relieved, she was heavy footed, with heavy breathing and the intense feeling of hatred wracked her body. She was angry for so many reasons. She locked her bedroom door and it was three days before she emerged.

Isabella was a changed person. People saw it in her eyes. Her eyes were dead and her stare haunting. Meanness traveled in her blood throughout her entire body. She spoke to no one. It was several weeks before she returned to the **Red Garter** and all the employees were suddenly afraid of her and kept their distance unless it was business. She seldom came out of her office at the restaurant or out of her bedroom in her home. Meanwhile she continued her journey in the mirror and growing more full of hate and fat from junk food left at her bedroom door. The maid and cook knew never to disturb her and only responded to her needs from notes left under the bedroom door. And now Isabella only wore the flowing caftans. Gone was the makeup, the manicured nails, the coifed hair.

The mirror was her only friend and enemy. She watched Marta slain by the black limo. She saw Salem disappear into the forest. Many times she saw the mansion explode. And several times the image of Excaliber eaten by the shards of light. She began reading the tarot cards again and their telling was always of doom and gloom. Consumed by sadness and a broken heart, the transformation of Isabella was frightening.

Frank had come by the house many times never to be received. Her telephone remained in disrepair and she showed up less and less at the **Red Garter**. Important business associates tried to maintain contact, but to no avail. There were debts and bills to be paid, but Isabella did not want to be bothered or even want care anymore. As those that had grown to love and respect her drifted away, as the **Red Garter** was failing with locked doors to the tourists and regulars, it was thought that Isabella Amadour Smithers was no longer.

Completely drained of emotion and feelings, Isabella tried to stay away from the mirror. She would sleep for hours and hours, constantly dreaming of the images that kept presenting themselves to her. Her sleep was never restful. When she would awake, it would be only a short time before she would find herself at the mirror once again.

Looking haggard and much older than her years, she sat before the mirror again. She never even noticed how bad she looked for all she wanted to do was see more. With Zomba in front of her and the snake's eyes wider than usual, but very still, the next image that appeared only made her anger grow deeper.

There before her was the image of Bill with a beautiful younger woman caressing him as she unbuttoned his shirt. The image was very clear, but she could not make out the face of the woman as it was hidden pressed against his back. Then the woman threw her head back in laughter and it was plain that it was Jazz.

Isabella slammed her fist against the mirror, breaking it but not shattering it. The cracks only made the scene before her more bizarre to her mind than what she was viewing. A blood curdling scream arose from deep in Isabella's throat that brought the maid banging on her bedroom door.

Refusing to answer, somehow Isabella shouted that she was fine and that she had stubbed her foot on the chair. Isabella had never before felt the wrath and anger she was overcome with now. The sight of Bill and Jazz fondling one another threw Isabella into action.

She sat on the edge of the bed and planned her next move.

It took Isabella almost a week to pull herself together. She called for her maid to have the telephone fixed, and then proceeded to make many calls to her hairdresser, her banker, her lawyer and set in motion meetings with each. She had many of her better outfits sent out for cleaning, had the maid polish her best Italian shoes, and pampered herself with only the best soaps and creams. She ate only nourishing salads and steak fixed by the cook to her liking and would sit in the dining room eating alone and barely speaking. The whole while her mind was racing to plot and plan revenge on any and all that had ever crossed her.

On the tenth day, Isabella unlocked the front door to the **Red Garter** and was shocked to see no one was there and it was lunchtime. The place was a mess. Dirty dishes with dried food remained on the tables and bottles of expensive wines were opened and scattered about. The main dining room was dark with the drapes pulled closed. The phone was ringing and the machine was flashing with many messages. The bar was full of drink glasses with liquor half consumed. She slowly walked down the hallway to her office to find the door wide open and papers strewn about. The safe was still closed, but someone had jimmied open the locked drawers of her desk.

She then walked to the kitchen and called out, but no one answered. She approached the closet that led to the *Back Door*, but just as she was about to open it, she was aware that someone had entered the kitchen behind her. Feeling their presence, she turned and was surprised to see Creaky.

"What has been going on here?" she screamed at him.

"Isabella, it is so good to see you. Where have you been? We were all worried, but no one seemed to be able to get through to you. Are you alright?" Creaky had a worried look upon his face, but his voice was very calm.

"Well, I'm here now. Never mind about me, I insist you explain this mess. And who had the right to enter my office, pry into my belongings? Where is everybody? You better have one hell of an answer for what I am seeing!"

Creaky approached her slowly and asked if they could sit in her office and talk? As Isabella took a seat at her desk, Creaky remained standing in front of her.

"It's like this," he began, "some of the regulars was pissed off that the place was, shall we say, not up to par. The chef quit when he didn't get paid. Some of the best girls just left and a couple of us tried to keep the place going. Frank did the best he could to keep the riff raff out, but a few nights ago it was more than we could handle and the cops shut us down. We tried to contact you over and over, but it was like you disappeared. The maid told me when I came by the house that you had left town. We couldn't get an answer on the phone and the cops said the only crime was that the **Red Garter** was becoming a dump and a health hazard." He then handed Isabella a newspaper with the story headlined by "New Orleans' Best Restaurant Is No More."

Isabella slumped back into the chair. She could feel her blood begin to boil. She glared back at Creaky, told him to go back out front and lock the door again and come back.

In spite of Isabella's fury, she softened when Creaky returned. The next four hours were spent checking out what damage had been done to the restaurant literally and then discussing what needed to be done and in what order to pursue getting the **Red Garter** functioning again. They made calls to cleaning companies, the linen supply company, put in calls to see what chefs may be available, calling some of the wait staff, ordering liquor and supplies.

All the while they worked shoulder to shoulder, Creaky could tell and plainly see that Isabella had changed. Gone was the warm charm, the pleasant smile, the soft voice. The lines on her face were deep and her eyes had no life. Even the way she smelled had changed. Although Isabella had done a remarkable job of cleaning herself up, the make- up was not perfect, and she spoke with a mean sounding voice. Creaky could not help but notice that Isabella had gained a lot of weight and was not wearing it well. She was making demands, and refusing to listen to any suggestions. Creaky was told to shut up and do as he was told. By the end of the day, he had a list of things to do and she wanted them done immediately with no excuses. His last command was to bring Frank to the office NOW.

"I'm sorry that isn't possible, Madam. Frank got into a scuffle with a couple of the regulars when they couldn't get into the *Back Door* for a weekly card game. Before blowing the cover on them and the place, he brought the fight in here and that's why so much of the furniture is broken. He ended up in the hospital when one of the young cops who didn't know who he was hit him so hard on the head with his club that Frank was sent to the hospital with a bad concussion. I think he'll be okay. I checked on him, but ya know he's an old man. Can't take a blow like that anymore."

"Alright then, tend to that list. I'll be here for several more hours. Call me and let me know how you are doing and don't let anyone of those ass holes that have made a fortune off this place give you any shit, understood?" Isabella gripped Creaky's arm hard, digging her fingernails into his flesh and pushed him out the office door.

As soon as she was alone in her office, she perused her desk and all the papers that lay about. When she reached down to the desk drawer that held the album with all her clippings and pictures and could not find it, she frantically looked everywhere in her office. It was nowhere to be found and a rush of panic trying to remember all that was in it flooded her mind.

Near tears and drained of any strength she had mustered in her arrival back to the restaurant, she went out to the bar and looked for the scotch she drank. Not finding any of the Johnny Walker Blue, she settled on a full glass of cheap Bourbon. She then returned to her office to find Creaky standing in the corner.

"I'll bet you have been looking for this," he smiled?

There Creaky stood holding out the leather bound album in both hands.

"Where did you get that," she yelled at him?

"I knew this was important and I didn't want anyone else to see it, so it has been in my possession since you left. I could feel the place was in trouble and I knew you were too. So I am the one that went through everything and found this. And I found the safe combination and made sure nothing was touched. The book with everyone's names and debts, the favors, all of it is still there. You don't have to fear that anyone saw that either. I made sure of it."

"Why? And how did you know? That book in the safe. Only Bill and I knew about that. Did you look through that album? You had no right. That's personal Creaky. I'll have you put in jail or better yet….."

Isabella stared at him and then threw her hand in his direction him. He slumped to the floor. She then pointed her index finger at his head and he grabbed the top of his head and yelled in pain.

"Stop it Isabella. I'm your friend. I will protect you as I always have. You don't need to do this," Creaky shouted in great pain.

Isabella brought her hand back to her side and stood over Creaky watching him closely. As he began to arise, the pain was subsiding. Creaky looked at her and told her they had more to talk about than just the restaurant.

Isabella stepped back and then forward to give Creaky a hand in getting up. It was evident that both were shaken from what had just happened. It was Isabella who spoke first, "What do you mean you have protected me as you always have?"

"I suppose it is time for me to tell you who I really am," he responded, and then stated, "I've always been there. From the time Electra entered your life, I was assigned to guard you. She feared Excaliber and his power and you were so young then. You had yet to understand what you could do. So my job was to watch you; see the extent of what you could do and be there if Excaliber harmed you."

"But I first laid eyes on you that first time I came to the **Red Garter**. I never thought you were anything else than an employee. Did Bill know you knew who I was?"

"I always suspected that your husband was aware of my watching you and just chalked it up to attraction. It was right before he died that I told him the whole story."

Isabella took her seat behind the desk and began quizzing Creaky about what he was saying. "So, okay, you know that I belonged to the society, that I had powers I was taught to control and why I was at the mansion. Were you there also?"

"Yes, I was there the whole time trying to keep out of sight and do certain chores for Excaliber that he demanded. I cooked the meals and did general housekeeping and he was satisfied to think of me as just his employee. I never told him who I was or why I had applied for that job."

"I know you have been seeking the mirror for answers to your past life and I know that you see me, but don't know who I am. I am the figure that you can't see a face.

I am the one who escorted you to the mossy field. I am the one who helped you get away. What I did not suspect was that Zomba was capable of destroying Excaliber or that you could implode that mansion."

Isabella was at a loss for words. The day had been very long and she was reeling from the work and now all she was being told.

"Are you a member of the society too," she finally asked?

"Not in the same respect as the rest. I met Salem a long time ago. We'd see each other occasionally and she began to trust me enough to tell me about her life. Then she took me to meet Electra. THAT was quite an experience. But I think the timing was right after Marta was killed and before Electra came into your life. Electra had interviewed me so many times and I guess she thought I'd be an asset to her. So I was suppose to be this dumb hard-working servant in the background and report to her. When your initiation was to begin, that's when I went to the mansion."

"So you know about the potion?"

"On that last day you were at the mansion and before hell began, I had reported to Electra that I sensed you were going to do something drastic. She told me to gather up as much of the potion as possible, be sure that I gathered any of your belongings that tied you to the mansion, and grab Zomba in the box at the first sign of problems.

With Zomba's wrath, I wasn't sure I could get to that box, but through the flames I was guided by the snake eyes to save him and just made it out one of the side doors before the house blew up. It was I that managed to get you all that money that you would need when you returned to the Quarter. It was I that found Salem after Excaliber banished her from the mansion. Together Salem and I went to the camp where Electra was and made plans for you. We loved you. We feared you. We knew you would be in dire need of help. It was your destiny. And mine."

"How did you know about the mirror? And exactly what did you tell Bill about me?"

Creaky now poured each of them a tumbler of whiskey. "Here drink this, you may need it."

Isabella sat quietly sipping the alcohol and listened without interrupting Creaky.

Creaky was in complete control now of the situation and was prepared to tell her the story.

He had already explained how he came to know Salem, Electra and Excaliber, but now he shifted his thoughts to Bill Smithers. He explained how he had met Bill and had taken a job at the **Red Garter**. The restaurant was thriving, he needed additional help, but he told Isabella that the restaurant was only making it financially because of the *Back Door*. Bill had gotten into some debt and the *Back Door* solved his problems. However the restaurant reached its highest approval once Isabella joined the staff. He shocked her more by telling her that her life was revealed to Electra and that the meeting with Bill and her falling for him and eventually marrying him was all part of the grand plan. After the mansion and witnessing your power, I knew that everything Electra had told me was absolute truth. The happiness that Isabella had found was deserved, but they all knew that it was temporary.

"So Bill knew of my powers," she asked?

"Let's just say, everyone who came in contact with you your whole life knew there was something special and powerful about you. It went beyond your beauty and intelligence. For example I remember there was this influential high-society dame that used to come into the restaurant for lunch with a bunch of other sharply dressed women. Everyone knew you did not like her just by your demeanor. But the day you rose a finger and pointed it at the waiter who was serving the table and he suddenly dropped the entire tray of food in her lap, I had to smile. When you did not fire the waiter, it confirmed by suspicions."

Isabella could not subdue the laugh that arose and she snapped her fingers while winking at Creaky.

"And the mirror, how do you know about that, she asked?

"I am in constant contact with Electra and she told me that is what you would eventually do because so many things would be confusing in your mind. That too is why I had to save Zomba. You would not see those images without the snake eyes."

"So where is Electra. And Salem? Can I see them?

"No. When Electra made the deal to take Sharon's baby to raise in the society, it was only with approval of the council that none of them have any physical contact with you. They are all old now. Much older than you can imagine. They are weak now. If I was to take you to them, it would mean their demise. Certainly death."

"Ok, Creaky, I only have one more question. Tell me what Bill knew and didn't know. And I'll know if you are lying. Did you know that Bill was having an affair with Jazz," she asked?

"That's two questions, Isabella, but I will tell you the truth."

Bill had been aware that Isabella had a past that included some involvement with a cult that had troubled her. Her reluctance to ever speak of herself was undeniable and he loved her enough to accept who she was whatever. But Bill was also aware that Isabella always seemed on guard and had this power of influence to make people do what she wanted. She practiced it on him all the time. It had been Isabella's insistence on keeping every detail written in his book of favors. Usually it was just an accounting of monies that exchanged hands, but now the book contain information that would prove disreputable and damaging. Bill was impressed by Isabella's insight and knowledge of people. She always seemed to know what would happen before it happened. After a while he did not question it, but took advantage of it. There were times Bill even thought that Isabella actually made her predictions happen. He would kid her about being a witch. She would always laugh and tell him she was and that he was under her spell.

"It was me that held Bill's head when he collapsed that day. I knew he was dying and that you would not get there in time. He could barely speak, but he was conscious and he kept saying your name over and over. I tried to reassure him that you would be okay and that you had many that would protect you. I explained that you really were a witch and that I was one of your guardians. I am known as Blalock and Frank Culotta is Baalam."

Isabella now laughed a hearty laugh, threw back her head and stared at the ceiling. When her head turned back down, she glared at Creaky and said, "And Jazz was fucking my husband, right?" The voice that came from her sounded loud, strained, raspy and deep. Enough so that all Creaky could say was, "yes!"

"We have work to do, Blalock," Isabella groaned, "tell Baalzebub, or whatever name it was that you called him, to meet us here tomorrow at 10:00 p.m. I don't care if he is still in or out of the hospital. Tell him to get here."

With that Isabella picked up the black book and waved Creaky out the door.

Isabella had a lot on her mind when she finally crawled into bed that night. First and foremost was Jazz. Now that the restaurant was going to be fully functional again, she would call all the employees and tell them when to return to work. Her first phone call would be to Jazz.

Part Two

Chapter FIVE

The Trio's Progeny of Doom

"Jazz, honey, this is Isabella calling. I want you to come back to work full time starting next week. It will take that long to get everything cleaned up and shining once again. I'll be at the restaurant all day from this point on shouting orders to workmen and distributors, but I don't need you until then. Will that be a problem?" Isabella was using her most sweet voice that actually was concealing her venom.

Jazz's response was she was thrilled to be coming back to work and would be there with bells on. Isabella hung up the telephone and stared into the mirror. She placed Zomba between her hands, closed her eyes and cast her spell.

Isabella's next call was to the Governor. Now her voice was harsh and hateful. She had no problem getting directly to him through his private number, but he seemed startled at the sound of her voice.

"What can I do for you, Isabella," the Governor asked?

"I'm holding a book in my hand that contains every detail of your misconduct and the entire story about Sharon. Also listed is the long outstanding debt you have owned Bill and I am calling it in. I need those funds to get the **Garter** up and running again now and I am giving you 72 hours to pay your debt to me in cash or I go to the newspaper and that surely will be the end of you in this town forever. Do you understand what I am saying? Do you know for a fact that I will do exactly what I am saying? This is not a threat, Governor, it's a promise." Isabella gave him no time to respond to her demand and slammed the phone back down into its cradle.

Then she turned to the mirror and Zomba and cast another spell.

As Isabella continued turning the pages of the book and noting the names of those that she had recorded their deeds, debts and scandalous ways, she could sense those old feelings of her power flowing through her veins. But this time she was not going to use her better side to control them. It was as though the teachings of Electra, and even Excaliber, were telling her that she had to only use her power with caution. She easily put those teachings out of her mind. With confidence that seemed to be coming from the marrow of her bones and with thoughts of revenge, she continued making her calls.

Next on the list was the Bishop. Once again Isabella spoke in honey voice and while she waited on hold for him to pick up his telephone, she plotted what to do.

"Why Isabella, so good to hear from you. How have you been? We were upset at what was happening at the **Red Garter** and no one seemed to know where you were or what was going on. I know you have had to face a lot and I was truly concerned." The Bishop was also using *his* honey voice.

"That's so good of you to care, sir. And that is why I called. I am in need of some counseling, but don't wish to come to you there. Would it be possible for us to meet in my office say one day next week….at your convenience of course?" Isabella had no intention of meeting with him, but in this way she might be able to glean his schedule.

Per usual the Bishop was full of himself and spouting his busy life explaining that he was in such demand of his time, but for her he would see what he could arrange. Would it be possible to give her a call back to set something up after his secretary checked his itinerary? "This week is out of the question. I have to be in Shreveport for a meeting over this weekend. But surely after that, I can find some time."

"Of course sir, I look forward to your call and especially our meeting," Isabella attempted to sound wounded so that he would comply.

As Isabella took some notes, she placed a call to Creaky and told him she needed him to go to Shreveport this weekend and she would get back to him with the details. She needed to know exactly where the Bishop would be staying in Shreveport and that would take a little research. Once again Isabella held Zomba and looked deep into the mirror.

The last starred name in the book was Charles DuCote. She had never trusted him and knew by suspicion that he may have been instrumental in Bill's death. She was not sure how, but Bill had alluded to the fact that DuCote was putting a lot of pressure on him right before he had collapsed. She was sure it was money, but there was no record of any debt. Plus Bill had been adamant about leaving any comments in regard to DuCote out of the book. Although Isabella knew not to question Bill, she watched DuCote with special interest every time they came in contact. This would involve a lot more research and she would set upon that once the **Red Garter** was running smoothly. Perhaps Frank or Creaky could fill in some blanks.

There were a few more names in the book that would also take some nosing about, but for now, Isabella's plate for revenge was full. "One thing at a time," she said out loud to herself.

The next few days were a blur of activity getting the **Garter** ready for its re-opening. It felt good to be back in familiar territory and work was putting the glow back into her cheeks and her eyes burned with determination. The days were long, but her nights were longer. She would return home, take a light supper and head to her bedroom where she worked into the wee hours to put her plans in order.

It was good that Frank was back at her side and doing her bidding along with Creaky. She was compelled to trust them completely now and neither of them ever questioned her instructions or asked any questions. They were her true servants. They would be rewarded someday.

She had located the hotel that the Bishop was registered in for his trip to Shreveport. All of the employees would be returning early Monday morning for a staff meeting. The bar at the **Red Garter** was now fully stocked thanks to the money from the Governor.

That was a shame what had happened to him. According to the newspaper account the Governor was alone on a walk to an unknown destination when he was beaten and robbed. His skull had been bashed in with a blunt instrument that was lying next to his bloody body. His wallet was found nearby empty of contents. There were no suspects. After questioning his family and friends, no one seemed to know what the Governor was doing alone so late at night by himself in the Quarter. That was not like him at all for he always surrounded himself with his cronies or guards. The family had posted a reward for any information in regards to the crime.

Isabella had clipped the story from the newspaper and pasted it in her scrapbook with a look of satisfaction upon her face.

She told Creaky that the Bishop was staying at the Hilton in downtown Shreveport and had a suite with an adjoining room. He would be arriving late Friday night and not scheduled to leave until Monday morning. She told him to take care of the business they had discussed.

Isabella then turned her attention to her notes on the staff meeting. It would be the first time she would be seeing Jazz since the sighting in the mirror. She could hardly sleep that night in anticipation.

The **Red Garter** was set to open for lunch and dinner that Monday. Few details needed to be attended to and the place was ready for tourist and regular customers. The chef was busy back in his kitchen with two new sous chefs to help and Isabella had hired three new bartenders and two new wait staff expecting a crowd based on dinner reservations that had poured in when the announcement was made of the re-opening. Isabella was in a particularly good mood and greeted the staff of old and new with great enthusiasm.

In the back of the small crowd that gathered around the bar at 9:00 a.m. stood Jazz dressed in black from head to foot and wearing what appeared to be a veil. As Isabella began the meeting with the usual instructions and new demands, she stopped herself in mid-sentence and called, "Jazz, is that you back there? What are you doing? Come up here and introduce yourself to the new members of our staff. Ladies and Gents, this is Jazz, our best hostess and one of my favorites. Come up here Jazz."

Jazz hesitantly moved past a few people and stood facing Isabella. "I can't, Isabella. I tried to call you over the weekend, but I could never get through. I'm here only because of that. I can't work here, at least for a long time." Her voice sounded as though she was on the verge of sobbing.

"What's with the veil, Jazz. Let me see your face," Isabella said?

Jazz lifted the veil slowly and Isabella did a remarkable Oscar- winning performance of holding back the outburst of laughter that welled in her and instead simply looked shocked and whispered to Jazz, "what happened?"

There Jazz stood with her face all disfigured with puss latent sores from her forehead to her chin. And she was crying.

"I don't know. I went to the hospital and they told me I must have had a bad reaction to something I ate. They gave me a lotion and a shot and told me to stay out of the light. I can't work like this. They don't know how long it will take to clear up. You will have to get someone else to man the lobby. I'm so sorry, Isabella. Can I leave now?"

"Of course, my dear. Get to feeling better. And call me, ok? Isabella patted Jazz on the shoulder and they all stood quietly until Jazz had left the lobby.

"What a shame gang. She is a very pretty girl and a plus to this restaurant, but she won't be able to work for I suspect a very long time. Now who here thinks they can step up to the plate and do a good job for me at the front desk?"

The **Red Garter** opened right on schedule and the lobby, bar and restaurant was doing record business. Isabella helped at the front desk through the lunch crowd with the waitress she picked to do Jazz's job just to give her some support, but mostly to accept the accolades of friends and regulars who were thrilled to be back eating at their favorite restaurant.

After taking a nap in her office, Isabella changed clothes into something fancier and prepared to see and greet the dinner crowd. Once again so many people were complimentary toward her and the **Garter** and commenting on how much they liked the new color scheme. The bartenders were working full tilt and doing such great business that Isabella feared they would run out of liquor. Isabella was delighted. When she could take a break from the front door, Isabella met with Frank in her office.

"So how did things go in Shreveport? I haven't seen Creaky most of the day. He's been very busy with other business, but he said the two of you managed to accomplish what I asked. Tell me what happened."

Frank asked if he could pour himself a drink and sat down on the couch. "You should have seen the Bishop's face when the photographers burst through the door. I wish I had had a camera myself, but I assume you plan to have the pictures all over the news and in the papers? The two boys we hired were fantastic. They started a conversation with the Bishop in the lobby and just as you predicted, it was only a few minutes before the three of them were in the elevator headed for the Bishop's suite. We waited about 20 minutes listening on the other side of the adjoining door and when we thought it was time, we signaled the photographers. It was over in a flash…..no pun intended." Frank was laughing at his own joke.

"I wish I could have seen that prick's face. But like you said, soon enough everyone will know." Isabella was beside herself with a combination of success and giddiness at the prospect that the church would finally find out what a pervert the Bishop was. "We can only hope that the Pope disrobes the S.O.B!"

When the last patrons left the restaurant, Isabella went back to her office and watched the late news on TV. There was no mention of the Bishop and his little encounter, but then again realized that the church was like a good old boys club and it might take a while. She could be patient as she held copies of the photos.

The next day would be much easier. Tuesdays in the restaurant business are slow. By Thursday things would be busy once again, so Isabella decided to go into the **Red Garter** late and instead focused on the book and re-checking names. There was still DuCote to deal with, but she needed more information.

There were unpaid debts from the Mayor and others. The *Back Door* needed to be dealt with and she wondered whether she wanted to get it up and running again. She would have to talk to Frank about that. He was still very reliable, but it was obvious that he was getting too old to handle the problems at the *Back Door*, let alone the *Big Bet*. Reinforcements would be necessary and after so much corruption on the police force, finding good "bad cops" was getting harder to come by in the Quarter.

Isabella also had found in re-opening the **Garter** that she had had to deal with a lot of new faces, some of which didn't know Bill personally, but only by reputation. That had made it more difficult because some of the distributors, the linen company, some of the contractors she had hired had not given her the respect she felt she deserved.

"They treated me like I was some dumb Broad, who didn't know the business world," she spoke out loud. It had pissed her off, but she knew better than to be anything but a lady and in spite of turning on the charm, she still felt as though she had to bow down to them. They did not know with whom they were dealing with and she intended to fix that one way or another.

Although she was alone in a world of men, none of them appealed to her in a sexual way. Occasionally she would eye a handsome man who looked and smelled of means, but her sexual drive seemed to have disappeared. Bill had been a wonderful lover and a good partner. She was sure she would never meet anyone like him again so why try? Since Bill's death, she had been approach by a few, some of them she even considered dating, but only for a fleeting second. Too much baggage, she thought. She called Creaky from her bed that night and made a date to go out to the mossy field early in the morning. She was running low on potion and she wanted to talk to him about DuCote.

Part Two

Chapter SIX

The Bishop and Isabella

Creaky picked Isabella up at 8:00 a.m. the next morning. It was foggy as they drove out to the field of moss and fungus. They parked the car at the end of the road that once led to the mansion and walked first in silence, then Creaky asked, "How'd you know the Bishop would go for those boys? Was it the mirror, or did you catch him doing the hanky panky with a little spanky?"

Isabella threw her head back and laughed. "Let me tell you a story, dear Creaky," she replied.

"I knew from an associate's son that the Bishop liked to park his car in a more secluded spot in Audubon Park. Apparently it was where a lot of perverts parked, but when the Bishop showed up they recognized his car and for their own reasons anyone there would disperse and leave. I decided one evening at dusk to see for myself. It took me awhile to locate the area, but I saw for myself the Bishop dressed in street clothes sitting in his car. He appeared to be alone, but then I noticed he kept ducking down and coming up and ducking down again. So I sat and watched from a safe distance. Then I saw a figure get out of the car and I figured the Bishop would leave. But a few minutes later a young man walked out from behind some trees and approached the car. They spoke for a few minutes and then the young man entered the back seat of the car. The Bishop crawls over the seat into the back and then I could not see anyone.

So I decide to sneak up to the window of the backseat and see for myself what is going on. I think I knew before I got there what I would see and I wasn't surprised. But you should have seen the look on that bastard's face when I tapped on the window and he turned to see my nose pressed up against the window. Startled by me, the next sensation the Bishop felt was the boy's teeth, which had grown to the size of a tiger, biting his swollen dick off. He shoves the frightened young man off with his screaming and the boy runs from the car fast as a blur. The Bishop is screaming "he bit off my dick," and sees blood gushing from his penis and scrotum. I watched for only a moment and then returned to my car. From there I could see some

other man running up to the car, so I continued to view the sight from my front seat." Isabella was delighting in telling Creaky the story.

"Did that kid really bite his business off," asked Creaky?

"What happened next was so damn comical, that I wanted to get closer, but stayed in my car. The Bishop is now out of the car, still screaming and running around looking all over the ground. I could hear him telling the new arrival that some kid bit his dick off and threw it somewhere. "I'm bleeding to death! I need a doctor." Then I heard the new guy tell him, "you're crazy old man, there is no blood, there was no kid running away. I was watching from over there waiting for the right moment to approach you. Look down stupid, you can see you still have your dick. I thought maybe you and I might connect, but you must be on something. I want no part of you mister. Zip up your pants and go home before all of your yelling brings the cops."

Once the Bishop realized that his penis was still attached, he climbed back into his automobile and with the interior lights on in the now darken park, Isabella could see him looking about and his face was white and his expression was total fear. He slowly started his way out of the park with no headlights turned on. Isabella sat for another few minutes before starting her engine and conjured up the nightmares that the Bishop would be having for the next few nights in the safety of his bedroom. She could not help but laugh out loud.

"Isabella, that was a wicked thing you did," said Creaky.

"Let me finish the story," she replied, and continued on. " I waited a few days and then the Bishop received a package marked confidential and personal at the rectory. It had no other markings other than addressed to him and inside was a note that read:

"If you continue to pursue, it will be the end of you."

Inside a smaller box was a severed dick!

"Wouldn't you have loved to have seen that pompous man's face at that moment," Isabella asked Creaky?

Creaky reached down with both hands and felt his package, then looked at Isabella and said, "So that's how you knew that our set up at the hotel in Shreveport would work? I don't know exactly how you pulled off his hallucinations and dreams, or where in the world you got a severed dick, but I know you are capable of it. But I must admit I'm a little surprised at the extremes you are going to."

They had arrived at the edge of the pine grove and began scooping up the fungus that is the base of the potion. After collecting a few bags full, in silence, they began their walk back to the lane to the car.

"There's something I want you to do for me immediately, Creaky," Isabella broke the silence.

"Whatever you want, just leave my dick alone, okay?" he answered.

"I know that Charles DuCote was in some way responsible for Bill's death. I can't put my finger on it, and I need you to tell me everything you know about that banker, his dealings with Bill and anything you may have overheard. Then I want you to spend the next 48 hours nosing about any leads you might uncover and report back to me. Even if it seems trivial, I want to know everything about DuCote. Understood?"

Isabella and Creaky arrived back in the Quarter just in time to attend to the noon crowd for lunch. Isabella deposited the potion mixture behind a locked door in her office with plans to concoct later that day and refill the empty small vials that awaited at her home. There was only two bottles left, she downed one and reported to the kitchen to see what the chef was preparing.

After the dinner crowd had left, Isabella told the new hostess it had been a trying day and she was leaving early. She drove home to be greeted at the front door by her maid who seemed upset. After trying to make head or tail out of her babbling, Isabella had concluded that apparently a reporter had come to the house and was asking a lot of questions. He had called several times and had left his card. The maid hoped she had done nothing wrong. Isabella quieted her, told her she would attend to it and that she only wanted a salad to eat, a bottle of Riesling and not to be disturbed in her bedroom until morning.

After the maid brought her salad and the wine on a tray upstairs, Isabella locked her bedroom door and proceeded to her bath to make up several bottles of potion. When she had filled a couple dozens of the small bottles, she stored them in a hidden compartment behind the armoire and climbed between the satin sheets to fall into a deep sleep.

The next two days were uneventful at her mansion and at the **Red Garter**. There had been more messages from the reporter, but Isabella had continued to ignore them. Late that evening Creaky arrived at Isabella's office door with news he had gathered about DuCote. They settled onto the comfy couch with a bottle of wine to talk of his findings. The dinner crowd had left and they were about to lock the front doors, so they knew they would not be disturbed.

"So tell me everything I need to know about DuCote," she demanded.

Creaky took a deep breath and told her she would not like what she was about to hear and he feared she might do something stupid that would end up hurting her. He made her promise to hear the whole story and not do anything without discussing it with Frank and himself. She nodded in agreement, poured the wine and sat back.

"Our Mr. DuCote is an evil man and you may have met your match, Isabella. I had to do some real digging, make promises and call in a lot of favors, but I think you were right about his being responsible for Bill's death. It seems years ago when Bill wanted to buy the **Red Garter** that he was strapped for funds and being fairly new in town and with the good old boy system and corruption in this city, he wasn't making any progress. Every bank had turned him down. And getting another liquor license was going to be impossible unless he greased a lot of palms. DuCote worked at the bank, but he wasn't the vice president then. He was a lowly bank manager who worked 18 hours a day for small pay and no appreciation by his bosses. When Bill and DuCote met they took a liking to one another but there was nothing DuCote could do for Bill without approval from the big men in charge. Loans were passed out to men of means or connections and neither had either.

I don't know how much time past but they had remained friends. They would go out to some of the more sleazy bars and drink cheap drinks and watch the whores dance. Both men were frustrated by "the system" all the while Charles DuCote's wife, who was from one of the prominent families in the city, was pushing DuCote to get ahead at any means. She must have been a real bitch from what I gathered and it was no wonder that DuCote wasn't saddened when she kicked the bucket. There were rumors that she died mysteriously of some kind of poison, but nothing was ever proven. By then he had risen in ranks and his daughter was highly thought of in society because of her grandparents. But poor Charles was disliked by most except Bill. It was also rumored, and I was able to confirm this, that Charles DuCote made a lot of shady deals within the city with a lot of lawyers behind him to secure property in places he had inside information about from connections with different associates. He was the brains and means behind a lot of construction companies. He filtered money to politicians that were in his pocket and he controlled the man in charge of liquor in this city. That alone made him tremendously powerful…especially in New Orleans."

Creaky took a big gulp of wine and studied Isabella's face as she continued to sit quietly taking in every word.

"Go on, get to Bill," she said.

"With DuCote now in a position to help Bill and pulling all the necessary strings, Bill opened the **Red Garter** with the help of Charles DuCote. At first DuCote was just pleased that he had his own table at the **Garter** and it was held every night for him whether he came in or not. He never had to pay for anything and took advantage of Bill many times by bringing in large crowds of prominent people to enjoy the restaurant. He would saunter in at the lead and spend the night ordering staff about and generally showing off in front of those that he had asked to join him.

Bill was always picking up the tab for the whole thing. And it was costing him a pretty penny. So according to an old bartender I found that worked here at that time, he told me that the two of them got into it in the office. He wasn't sure, but he thought they had actually gotten physical with one another."

"How long ago was this," Isabella asked?

"It's hard to say when all of this took place, but if you know when the *Back Door* opened, you'll be able to pinpoint an approximate time. Apparently after their fight, DuCote was tired of Bill's complaining about money so he suggested a back door operation that would bring in plenty of money and make them both rich. The city has always been good about turning a blind eye to gambling and prostitution, so it seemed like a good idea. Especially with DuCote's connections and Bill's affiliation with the police and mayor back then. Of course it was a different mayor and police commissioner, but reputations are hard to come by and even harder to break."

"So the *Back Door* was DuCote's baby?"

"So the story goes," Creaky continued. "The *Back Door* has always been the money maker here, and when the *Big Bet* began, it soared. To tell you the truth, the reason the **Garter** almost failed and Frank got into that awful scuffle that nearly killed him, was because of the *Back Door*. I was glad you weren't here. It really got nasty with a bunch of men you know personally fighting over how things had changed with Bill's death and that you were not capable of running a smooth operation."

"Oh, I see," Isabella interrupted, "I'm just this woman who kept it together after we lost Bill, but it still wasn't good enough for them? Don't spare me the details as to who we are talking about, but for now, get back to what happened. We'll discuss that matter later."

Creaky took another big swallow of wine, stood up and now began to pace the office floor as he went on with his information. Isabella tried to put aside the fury that was rising to the surface, but focused on Creaky and watched as he paced and spoke.

"Bill did not want you involved with the *Back Door* which is why he kept it from you in the beginning. But the two of you were a duo of strong wills and even though I may have appeared at the time to always be in the background, I knew you would become his right hand man and that he would eventually include you. I think he knew you had powers over people and I know you could always control Bill. There were a lot of objections in the beginning to you taking any part, but you did your thing and those men trusted you."

"The girls that would perform any deed called upon behind the curtain were now substituted by the staff of girls you controlled. All of them liked the beauty and the class, but many of them complained about no more blow jobs. Your new rules made it impossible for them to have their fun with the whores and they would have to return to their wives or find other means for their sex drives. That was a real problem in the beginning. But the liquor was fine and the money was high stakes. That is really what they wanted and they could find whores anywhere. So in time things calmed down until one night when DuCote in a drunken foul mood made a remark that caused almost every man in the *Back Door* play quiet and stupid."

Now Isabella leaned forward on the couch. The intensity in which she was looking at Creaky made him grab his balls.

"DuCote was under the impression that he could say and do anything he wanted without consequences. He thought he was completely above the law since the law owed him a lot. He thought *everybody* owed him a lot, but even though people were afraid of him and his power, even the weakest man in the *Back Door* took offense to DuCote shouting at Bill that he was a leach, stupid and wouldn't have anything if it wasn't for him. He yelled at Bill, "while you look like a plum of society with that bitch wife of yours, live in a big mansion with servants and run a fine eatery, you never had to scratch and be shit on like me to get those things. I could shut you down tonight if I had a mind to and call in the debt you owe me."

"What happened and where was I when this took place?" Isabella asked.

"I can't remember exactly when it was, but I do know you had a headache and told Bill you were going home. You were not up to playing hostess in the *Back Door* and everything was in order. So you left around midnight and things didn't start happening until, oh it must have been somewhere around 3:00 a.m. DuCote was losing at the table and he had been drinking even more than usual. He was in a foul mood and everyone knew it, but no one cared why. Some of the members decided to leave not wanting to be involved. There became a mass exodus for the door after that. I hung around in case Bill needed any help and it took both Frank, me and two of the guards to get DuCote out of there. The last words I heard DuCote yelling at Bill was that he was going to pay him his debt."

"I went back into the restaurant to check on things. It was dark and all locked up, so I returned to the *Back Door* and asked Bill if he needed anything. He dismissed me and I started to walk down the alley toward the street. I was aware of a Lincoln coming down the alley from the other end, but really paid little attention. I rounded the corner and then I heard a shot. When I ran back around the corner Bill was lying on the ground grabbing his chest. The Lincoln was speeding in reverse back out of the alley. I tried to see who it was, but the headlights were blinding me to see the driver. I was more interested in if Bill had been shot.

He was conscious and gasping for air but I could not find any bullet hole. He leaned up slightly and said in a whisper, "I think I'm having a heart attack. Get help." I tried to get back into the *Back Door*, but Bill had locked it. So I ran back around the corner to the all night Deli and called for help. Then I ran back to Bill who was now ashen and losing consciousness. His last words to me was, 'Tell Isabella I know, it made no difference. I loved her.' And he died in my arms."

The two of them now became silent. Time seemed to stand still. Finally Isabella arose, went to the desk and picked up her purse and told Creaky she was going home.

She left without saying another word. Creaky locked everything up and he too left.

That night Isabella sat before the mirror with Zomba in her hands. The room was dark until the light from the jar suddenly glowed and the eyes appeared. "Zomba I command of you to show me the way to destroy."

It was announced on the morning news that a prominent vice president of an long standing bank in the heart of the city had been in a horrendous car accident that had left him paralyzed from the waist down. He was in serious condition with the story to follow.

Isabella knew the story. She did not need to find out any of the details. She simply waited for the rest of DuCote's fate.

Part Two

Chapter SEVEN

The Downfall

Charles DuCote spent several months in first the hospital, and then in a nursing home trying to recover from his injuries. His room was filled with flowers and cards when Isabella Smithers went to visit him.

DuCote's reaction to Isabella's visit was as phony as he was. Acting delighted to see her and portraying the image of the suffering victim but maintaining his dignity, he invited her to sit awhile and tell him the news from the **Red Garter** and the Back Room.

Not to be outdone in the acting department, Isabella was all sweetness and light with prayers for his recovery and that soon he would return to his former life. After a few pleasantries and good wishes, Isabella approached his bed, leaned down and whispered in his ear. When she stood back up she was pleased to see the look of fright upon his face. And then as a nurse came through his door, Isabella threw DuCote a kiss, a wave and the promise to come again to visit. She walked down the hallway of the nursing home with an extra light gate in her step. She could hear the nurse calling for an orderly to help her with this patient.

She later told Creaky what she whispered in Charles DuCote's ear. Creaky was not surprised when she said that she told him he would never recover, never walk again, and that his only way out of the misery he was in was to shoot himself in the head.

"I could hear him screaming as I left," Isabella laughed.

It would take another month before DuCote was released from the nursing home and sent home with a round- the- clock nurse, a therapist and an on-call doctor being the center of his life instead of his daughter Lyn.

It was Creaky that brought the newspaper to Isabella's office that morning that contained the story of the well-known bank vice president who shot himself in the head over depression brought on by a life-changing automobile accident. Funeral services to be private.

Isabella was finally feeling justified and satisfied in the fate of her enemies. With DuCote gone there were only a few left in the book that she needed to attend to, but all in good time. Meanwhile she was keeping busy with the restaurant and had even begun dating a businessman from Baton Rouge.

They were merely friends, but she felt he wanted to be more. Perhaps, maybe, but probably not. In the meantime he was a nice distraction and pleasant company. Isabella's concentration was now on the *Back Door* and refurbishing it to open once again. It had been months and patrons of the *Back Door* were forever asking her in private if and when it might be in operation once again. After a lot of consideration, she decided it might be good to have the extra income. Plus with several new restaurants in the Quarter giving her a lot of competition, it might even be necessary.

But Isabella was finding it to be an arduous task. Making phone calls to old friends in the construction business that she could trust to be secretive about the *Back Door* turned out to be almost fruitless. Many had either retired, left the city or simply did not want to work for her. Forced to do business with unknowns, she vetted them for reliability, prices and most of all loyalty to silence about the improvements. They were to do what they were told and ask no questions. To her chagrin so many of the ones that applied for the job were young and seemed rather arrogant. Obviously they did not want to take orders from a woman. When she was about to give up on the idea completely, she interviewed an owner of a new company in town that seemed as though he could comply with her wishes and better yet, spoke to her in a respectful way. "When can you start," she asked. "Today," he answered. She liked that.

The only thorn in Isabella's life was the hounding of the reporter who seemed determined to speak with her. He had been calling for months and had even stopped by the **Red Garter** hoping to see her. She had informed every employee of this reporter and told her employees if any of them let the reporter get to her, they would be fired. She placed the same buffer system at her house and put him out of her mind. That is until one afternoon as she left her house in the Garden District through the backdoor and found him standing in her courtyard.

"Who are you. May I help you? This is private property. You must leave." Isabella had no time for this intruder.

"My name is Jack Draper and I work for the Tribune. I've been trying to have a meeting with you for months. I want to do a story on you and about the **Red Garter**. It's come to my attention that you are a witch. Is that true?"

"Get off my property or I'll call the authorities. I have no intention of wasting my time with you or any of your accusations. If I am a witch, as you say, then you had better get the hell out of here before I set you on fire!" Isabella turned and ran back into the house.

She went to the phone and called the Tribune and asked to speak to the managing editor. When the receptionist said he wasn't available, Isabella simply said, "Put him on this phone immediately or the next call you will get will be from my lawyers."

There was a long pause and then a man's voice said, "This is Harry

Bordean, who is this?"

"My name is Isabella Smithers. I am the owner of the **Red Garter** and I want to know what you are going to do about a reporter of yours named Jack Draper who has been stalking me for months and just now I found him in my courtyard. I don't know what this is all about but he is making accusations and I will sue you for slander if you don't get this ass hole off my back."

"Now, I'm sorry what was your name, Miss Smith?" he calmly said.

"You heard me, my name is Isabella Smithers and I'm the owner of the **Red Garter** in the Quarter. I know you know the restaurant, but you don't know me. But I assure you that you will have my name embedded in your brain till the day you die if you don't get rid of that reporter." And with that she slammed down the phone.

As difficult as it was for Isabella to gather her wits, she called the maid and cook and told them what had just happened. She then told them if he came to the door, or called again they were to call the police. As soon as she arrived at the restaurant she called Frank and Creaky to the office and told them to find out who this creep was so that she could deal with him in her way.

Going about her business, she turned her attention to the young electrician who was subtracted by her new contractor. He didn't say much, which she liked, as they stood over the schematics and the drawings of what the *Back Door* was to be. She could not help but notice that he stood particularly close to her and smelled of after shave she thought quite pleasant. He appeared to be about 30, muscular and had a golden tan.

"Where did you get that tan? It isn't from being indoor wiring buildings, I'll bet," she asked?

He seemed a little embarrassed by her comment with a flush of pink coming to his face. He stepped back and said, "No Madame, I like to water ski on the Pontch ever chance I git."

"Oh I detect the accent. You must be from the Bayou, no?"

"Yee Madame, from down Lafourche Parrish. Got me a boat and I spend a lot of free time fishin' and skiing. Friends like me cause my boat."

"Well, I'll like you if you do a good job. OK? How long do you think this is going to take?"

"Be done with this here job in about a week, maybe sooner." He replied.

"Then I'll leave you to your work. Are you doing this alone? Isabella asked?

"When you good like me, you don't need no one," he smiled.

The week spread to a second week. The work was being attended to every time Isabella entered the room, but she was convinced that when he was in there by himself he must not be working. She suspected he drank on the job because the sweet smelling after shave now smelled of whiskey most of the time. She decided to call the foreman of the company she had hired to ask a few questions.

The foreman of A.S.A.P Company, Claverie Bueche, convinced Isabella that Harmon was a good man and would do a good job. That it was taking longer according to Harmon because the building was full of such old wiring. In order to get the lights the way she wanted them over the tables, he was having to replace everything. "Should be done by next week," he said.

"Well I have the painters and carpet men coming next week. Get someone in here to help him. It has to be done if I'm going to open it on schedule. Next week and not a day longer." Isabella hated dealing with strangers. She would have paid double to get some of her old crew back.

That night the restaurant was closed for a private party that the staff had been prompted to and given orders to follow to the letter. Isabella was going to dinner at Mulate's and kick up her heels with some dancing and laugh once again with Joseph.

He was back on business from Baton Rouge and she surprised herself at how giddy she felt at the idea of being with him again.

After considerable amount of primping and powdering, Isabella looked in the mirror and threw herself a kiss. She looked damn good for a woman who was aging fast and the years were beginning to take their toll on her. But she cleaned up nicely and looked great in the new black slacks that hugged her now more slender body. All of the hard work she had been putting in and refusing to test all of the chef's dishes was beginning to pay off. "Could romance be in my life again," she thought?

Right before she started to leave there was a telephone call. She refused it at first but when the maid said it was the restaurant calling and it was an emergency, she could not refuse the call.

"Yes, what's the problem?"

"Isabella, this is Creaky. We've had a fire in the Back Room. You'll have to come down here and speak to the Fire Department Chief. He's asking all sort of questions and wants to speak to only you. I'm sorry."

Isabella quickly called Joseph and didn't get an answer. She then called Mulate's in hopes that Joseph might be there. They were of no help and she had no alternative then to head to the **Garter** and try to call Joseph later.

Arriving at the **Red Garter** she had to park two blocks away because of the engines that had apparently put out the fire and were still cleaning up, had just begun to reel in the hoses. Any fire in the Quarter has a fast respond time due to the age and closeness of the buildings. The hardest job for the fire truck is managing to get through skinny roads, traffic, let alone down a dead-end alley. But the restaurant seemed to be fine and the fire was contained only to the *Back Door*. The problem was that the Fire Chief wasn't aware of the *Back Door*. He had a lot of questions as to the fact that it was listed as a storage area and he could see that wasn't true. What was the room used for?

The old Fire Chief would have never quizzed Bill or Isabella, but just like everyone else in Isabella's life it was like "out with the old and in with new." Chief Post had played many poker hands at the *Back Door*. This new young fire chief was by the book for his reports and being very invasive with his questions.

Isabella's evening was ruined. So was the *Back Door*. Turning on charm, using her power, lying, nothing was going to make this Fire Chief and his questions go away.

She tried to convince him that business was so good that they were expanding the restaurant and that she had hired a young electrician to do all of the new wiring. She reported the company's name and its owner, plus Harmon's name. She didn't know Harmon's last name. After a couple of hours had past, the fire trucks were gone and there was just the smell of lingering smoke and lots of water all over the place as a reminder of what had happened. That and a destroyed *Back Door*.

Isabella went to her office and tried to call Joseph once again. With no answer, she decided to head back home and hoped that he would call her.

The next day the Fire Chief came back to the restaurant to inform Isabella that the company she had hired to do the construction and the subcontractor Harmon were not licensed in the state or the city and that he felt from evidence that the fire had been intentionally set. If that were the case, her insurance would not cover damages. Once more the entire structure would now have to be inspected and if more problems were found, he could condemn the building.

For the first time in a very long time Isabella missed Bill. This was too much. She was exhausted trying to get back to a good place after ridding herself of her enemies. She was anxious to get on with her life. Perhaps with Joseph, but definitely with the **Red Garter** *and* the *Back Door* functioning full capacity. This was a setback she wasn't sure she could handle.

The next two weeks were filled with meetings at her home informing the staff that if indeed the **Red Garter** was able to re-open, she expected their loyalty and return to their duties. She was still waiting on the bureaucracy of inspectors, insurance companies and lawyers to settle on her claim so that the work could begin on repairing the damage done by the fire. The entire building would have to be re-painted and a lot of water damage was done to the kitchen. The *Back Door* was still a guessing game as to its future.

When Isabella was permitted to return to the **Garter** and peruse the damage, she had been astonished at the extent of needed repair. She began looking for a reputable construction company that would do the work on the contingency of all the reports she was waiting for. That job was more involved than she anticipated simply because she was determined to find a good company to do the work and those were busy with so many projects that she could not get any company to agree. She set in motion getting the permits and that would take days. Plus permits would not be issued until the Fire Department and the insurance companies agreed to the reconstruction. The paperwork and the feeling that no one was interested in attending to business in a timely manner was depressing Isabella even more. Meanwhile the income she depended upon was disappearing along with any savings she had accumulated.

Isabella sat at her desk in her bedroom and consulted the tarot cards. With each turn her mood bounced from sadness to anger. The cards were revealing nothing but bad omens. Even consulting Zomba had proven disaster because the light never appeared and the eyes never opened. She had never felt more alone. The friendship with Joseph had dwindled to polite phone conversations and nothing more. He was sympathetic about her situation, but was unable to support her in any way due to his own schedule and business dealings. However Isabella was convinced in her mind that he just did not want to get involved. His excuses had become more vague.

The bad news came on the Monday of the third week. She was informed by mail that the building was condemned and that construction would have to be the removal of the structure from the property. That was followed by the report that the structure had been intentionally set upon by fire and therefore any insurance would be null and void. If Bill had not outright owned the building and its contents that she had inherited, she would have been responsible for any and all of those debts. To think that was the only redeeming value was little consolation.

The lawyers were fighting a good fight with City Hall, but now it was looking less formidable. It became apparent to Isabella that it was a lost battle and perhaps she needed to take out her fury on those responsible for her loss in her own way. A call to Frank and Creaky to come to her mansion resulted in her demand to find Harmon and the owner of A.S.A.P. and report back to her.

Isabella was convinced that if the fire was intentional, then one or both of them would pay.

It took a few days, but Frank returned to Isabella's home and reported that he had found Harmon working an electrical job in Algiers. Mr. Bueche was called unexpectedly out of the country, but with further investigation Frank was sure he was on some extended vacation living it up on a friend's yacht.

Isabella could not help but notice that Frank did not look good. His hands shook and his speech was more slow than usual and she inquired as to whether he was feeling all right.

"That hospital stint did me more harm than good," he reported. "They have me on this medication that makes me shake and I can't seem to gather any strength. I'm getting up there you know and all I want to do is sleep. I've lost about 20 pounds and not interested in eating. The doctors keep chalking it up to my age and that it would take a while longer to get back to par. I think they are lying to me."

"Frank I'm sorry you are not well. You should have said something sooner. I can see that you are worn out. Take some time off from all of this and call me when you are feeling better. I think Creaky and I can handle everything from this point on. Now where exactly is that Harmon prick working."

Frank handed Isabella a slip of paper with an address, thanked her for the time off and left. Isabella went to her city map to find a route to the location on the slip of paper. She was unfamiliar with that part of the area of New Orleans, but headed out in her car alone to seek it out. It had been an easy drive and she immediately saw the van that Harmon drove parked in front of a small brick building with a sign that read *"Carmichaels Repair."* She parked her car and just watched for a while.

She could hear activity coming from the building, but could not see anyone. She hesitated to approach the building, but wanted to see for herself if Harmon was there. She decided not to take a chance and would come back the next day.

Once again she parked her car several car lengths from the white van, but this time she went inside the open garage door. She could see that it was an auto repair shop and could hear the sounds of pounding hammers and then she heard what sounded like a blowtorch. She crept past some cars and walked toward the sound. There was Harmon standing in front of an open fuse box with his back to her. She bumped into a large container on the floor that was filled with some sort of liquid other than water. It was at that moment that Isabella decided her revenge.

She knocked the container over causing the liquid to run toward Harmon. He had on a welding mask and had not heard any sounds. She then walked through the liquid and stood right behind Harmon. He must have sensed someone there because with blowtorch still in hand and electrical wires falling onto the floor and connected in a worn way to the fuse box, she simply reached past him and threw a big switch into the up position just as he turned toward her.

Sparks began to fly. Harmon looked down and saw the liquid and quickly looked back into Isabella's eyes which shone red with evil. At first there was little reaction, but then the liquid began to catch fire and Harmon stood in complete fright fixed in his position. Isabella then smiled at him, turned and calmly walked away. Just as she approached the entrance to the garage door she heard a small explosion. She kept walking slowly toward her car.

On her return to her home in the Garden District she contemplated her next move. It was purely by luck that her book and album had been taken home and not left in the office. It had been her nightly ritual to crawl into bed and turn the pages of both in these last months. All the while plotting and planning. With the fate of Jazz, the Bishop, the Governor, Charles DuCote and now Harmon, she was turning her attention toward the lesser of her enemies. "Might as well rid myself of all of them," she said to herself. First on the list were the names Creaky had given her that had made disrespectful comments about her while at the *Back Door*. "Pussy men that have no guts to say to my face what they think, but use me as fodder for their fun remarks to show off in front of other pussy men. None of them should have been given the time of day by me."

Isabella was out of control now. She would show them. And thus began a week- long melee of strange events happening to many of New Orleans most prominent citizens. Letters and pictures were sent to C.E.O's wives that resulted in costly divorces. The Mayor's newly constructed home in Plaquemine Parish suddenly caught fire that caused a scandal regarding funds in its building. The headlines hounded him daily with questions as to where the funds came from. Two children of another prominent citizen were missing One of the largest law firms in the city was now connected to a mob organization operating out of Chicago. And as Isabella checked off each name in the book, she was surprised by her lack of satisfaction. She felt nothing. Certainly not remorse.

Keeping mostly to herself and holed up in the mansion drained of funds in her savings account, she only left the house to sell a piece of jewelry or incognito she would ride the trolley to the Quarter to buy a *Lucky Dog* from a vender and sneak back home. The maid and cook had been let go and she rambled about the large mansion with all the drapes closed. Darkness was her best friend now. She spent hours with her bones, tarot and trying to get Zomba to open his eyes. She always carried her album with her now filled with newspaper accounts of the fate of her enemies.

Isabella only spoke to Creaky who would come frequently carrying bottles of liquor and some food items. It was Creaky she thought was ringing her doorbell and was shocked to open the door to face three police officers.

"Are you Isabella Amadour Smithers," asked the one in the forefront?

"Yes, I am," she answered.

"You are under arrest. You have the right to remain silent." The last words Isabella heard were, "You have a right to an attorney."

The Sinners of New Orleans

The Story of Isabella Amadour Smithers

Part Three

Chapter ONE

The Prosecution of Isabella

Isabella was interrogated for hours at police headquarters. She had placed a phone call to her lawyer who had yet to arrive. She sat motionless and quiet and they continued to ask questions with her only response was she wanted her lawyer and that was her right. She could not imagine what was taking so long for him to get there. His secretary said that he would be at the downtown precinct right away and yet the clock on the wall showed her it had been going on three hours. She remained silent.

Finally a young man entered the interrogation chamber and announced that he was representing Ms. Smithers.

Isabella looked up from her constant downward gaze to look at a stranger. She had never seen him before. "Who are you," she demanded to know?

"My name is Austin Devaraux and I am here to represent you. I am sorry to announce that Mr. Sussex and Mr. Stein are not available and they asked me to come down to get you through these preliminaries. I assure you that is all that these are. I spoke to the arresting officers and asked to see the charges. You'll be out of here within the hour. Now if you gentlemen would get Ms. Smithers a drink of water and leave us, I wish to consult. Give us 20 minutes."

The male and female officers arose, left the room and the female returned with a can of Coke. Isabella grabbed the can and within two swallows finished the entire can.

"Okay, Ms. Smithers…..may I call you Isabella….tell me in your own words exactly what happened and why you think you are under arrest." Austin appeared dapperly dressed, clean-shaven and his voice indicated confidence, but Isabella could not help but wonder just how old was this kid and where were her lawyers.

"Mr.Devaraux,….may I call you Austin"….(Isabella was being sarcastic), "you have to answer my questions first. Where is Peter or Harvey? I don't know you at all and I am only speaking to one of them."

"Ms. Smithers, they are on other cases and unavailable. Mr. Stein is out of town on his case and Mr. Sussex is in court right now. The office informed me of your predicament and asked me to fill in and to get you through with the judge, so we can get you out of here. The charges are rather numerous and include attempted murder. We have to wait for the night judge to come in and hear exactly what the prosecutor is going to present. I would have introduced myself earlier, but with all of the paper work they handed me, I was held up myself just going through those so I had a better understanding of what you were facing. You did not say anything to those officers, did you? It's important that you don't admit to anything." Austin was seated across from Isabella looking deep into her face.

"Look kid, I'm not stupid. I did not answer any questions and I don't know what you are talking about. Attempted murder? Who do they say I tried to kill? And what other charges? This is a travesty. I don't know what I am doing here, but young man you had better get me out of here."

The female officer returned to the interrogation room and announced that Ms. Smithers was going to have to go to a holding cell until the judge arrived. Austin assured Isabella that she would be home in a few hours, that she should go with the officer and that he would see her in court.

As Isabella sat in a holding cell alone, she could see a larger cell across the hallway with several people all sitting and waiting. They appeared to be a cross section of the types of people that roam the Quarter in various modes of dress and degrees of intoxication. She asked an attending officer if she could go to the bathroom and asked if she could have her purse back. The young officer returned to the cell carrying her purse and as she riffled through it looking for a lipstick and comb, she noticed that things had been examined and placed back in a shoddy manner.

As she stood in the bathroom with the officer at the inside door watching her, Isabella stared at herself in the mirror. Her hair was disheveled, she had no makeup on and her clothes were at least three days old, wrinkled and smelling of body odor. "Fine way to face a judge," she thought.

After another long wait in the holding cell, finally the officer came to get her and escort her to the courtroom. There was Austin sitting on the left side of the aisle at a table facing the judge. Isabella took the seat next to him. At the prosecution table sat a league of three piece suited gentlemen and one lady all with open brief cases and avoiding Isabella's stare.

The judge arrived from his chambers and the proceedings began. By now Isabella's anger had been replaced by hunger and exhaustion. "This is just a preliminary to determine the charges. We will have plenty of time to consult afterwards. I will drive you home and after a good night's sleep, we will go over everything in the privacy of your home or at my office. Understand?" Austin was using his most sympathetic voice in a whisper.

Isabella now focused on the judge. She knew almost all of them from the restaurant or the *Back Door*, but this one was unfamiliar to her. She learned that he was a visiting judge brought in for this one hearing. That is when it dawned on her the seriousness of what was happening. They could not seat any judge that personally knew her for prejudicial reasons. She leaned over and asked Austin if that were the reason? He simply shook his head yes.

The judge, who was His Honor Joseph Feud, began to read the charges. Isabella became weak in her sitting knees at the long list that included extortion, bribery, illegal gambling, fraud, attempted murder and witchcraft. Even Austin gasped outwardly and stood to protest the charges.

"Your Honor, Mrs. Smithers is a respected member of New Orleans society and a highly respected restaurateur in the community. These charges are preposterous. I have had only a few minutes to peruse the charges in the document before you and can find no proof of any of them stated. Unless the prosecution can present any evidence that Ms. Smithers is guilty of even a traffic ticket, she should be allowed to go home."

With that said, the prosecutor stood and waved a bunch of papers loudly announcing that they had proof of her guilt and that copies of everything had been sent to Mr. Devaraux's office. They intended to prove all of the counts and because of the seriousness of the charges she should remain in the city jail to await trial without bail.

The judge asked Isabella to stand and make her plea. "I am not guilty of any charge, sir. I am a business woman in this community and have no connection with any of the charges you read. I am NOT GUILTY!"

The judge studied Isabella for a moment and then announced that the charges were of such corrupt and convoluted proportion that he had no alternative then to reprimand her to the city jail on a million dollars bail.

Isabella collapsed back into her chair as Austin began arguing that she proposed no flight risk, her reputation was spotless and the bail was inappropriate to the unproven charges. None the less, the gavel dropped and Isabella was taken back to jail. She could not even hear Austin's pleas to be strong and that he would see her the next morning.

The trial was to begin in seven weeks. Unable to produce the bail of a million dollars, she remained behind bars in a solitary cell with her only touch with the outside world being Austin and a few visits from Creaky. Creaky had been instructed to call upon certain individuals that owed Isabella in financial and favored ways, to come to her assistance. Most of that was in vain due to the headlines and news reports speculating and telling relentlessly the story of Isabella Amadour Smithers, The new New Orleans Witch.

Creaky proved himself once again her one true and faithful friend bringing her fresh clothes and personal items. When she asked him about Frank and why Frank had not come to see her, she was disappointed in Creaky's vague answers. Creaky had shut down the mansion and the restaurant as she told him to do. Austin had informed senior lawyers at the firm of the situation and they had determined that Austin should continue the representation as first chair and that they would assist him if Isabella agreed. She saw no other choice as it was clear that Peter and Harvey were not interested in helping her. In the seven weeks for the trial to begin, it was obvious to Isabella that the notoriety she was receiving in the daily newspapers and television news that people were distancing themselves. The price she paid for all those influential cronies that felt safe guarded with her locked up.

Deprived of the potion, her hair was beginning to fall out. Her complexion was sallow and her nerves shot. With no tarots, bones or even attempting to get Zomba's attention, she had never felt so all alone and bounced her emotions between depression and bone chilling anger. She plotted. She cried. She slept for hours on end or paced her cell. Sometimes when Creaky came to see her, he left scared at her catatonic state and other times he worried at some of the brash statements she made. He knew that Isabella was out of control. He did not have the heart to tell her that Frank had abandoned her and that last month was found dead in his apartment. Unknown causes were stated, but the death certificate read asphyxiation from internal complications.

Creaky was limited in what he could do. He sought out his connections with Electra and Salem, but they too had disappeared. He tried his hand at asking the paid-off cops that had always helped Isabella with duties at the *Back Door* for their assistance, but to no avail. He had conversations with employees and especially Jazz that did not produce any help or even good will toward Isabella. Creaky concluded that he alone had her back and without her orders and direction was bordering on worthless to her. So he did what he could for his boss and saw her as often as they would allow.

The restaurant was now dark, in disrepair and abandoned just like Isabella. The For Sale sign on the mansion lawn only drew tourists and gossips, but no offers to purchase. The lawyer fees had cleaned Isabella out and the trial had not yet begun. What was to become of Isabella's fate?

The night before the trial was to begin, the two sat in the visiting room not speaking but holding hands. Creaky had brought her the Chanel suit she requested and all the needs she had to make herself look as presentable as possible.

In the weeks preceding the trial date, Isabella had met with Austin daily answering his questions as best she could without being completely honest or divulging secrets. When the names of past enemies were thrown at her and about their relationships, she always said just enough to satisfy Austin with a modicum of truth and half truths. Knowing how important it was for him to have the whole story, she simply could not tell him everything without convicting herself. She never denied certain associations or knowledge that hurt her enemies, but never admitted to any involvement in their demise. She admitted to the *Back Door* activities and the gambling, but as far as Austin was concerned that was the only evidence that the prosecution had. Isabella was accepting that responsibility.

As for bribery she felt as though certain people did owe her and did pay her but always in favors. "I bartered favor for favor like everybody else in this town. If you know what you need and where to get it, you use that. So what?" was her reply.

Extortion and fraud was a joke as far as she was concerned and they couldn't possibly have any proof of that because there was none.

The attempted murder charge was the most damaging. It was Harmon that had gone to the police. That charge worried her and kept her awake at night. As Frank and Creaky had always done the really dirty work, she had taken that one on herself. In spite of taking great pains not to be seen at *Carmichael's Repair* shop, she had thought that her plan to eliminate him had worked. He should have gone down in electrocution, but she admitted to Creaky she did not actually witness his death. That was her biggest mistake and he had to do something about it.

But what worried Isabella the most was that Creaky was unable to find Harmon and finish the job. Although Creaky spent the better part of every day trying to find Harmon on a fishing boat or at work or at home, it was like he left the hospital and disappeared. Creaky understood that his main help to Isabella was to find him and truly make him disappear. Isabella was at a loss without her tarot, bones and Zomba to guide her and tell Creaky where to find Harmon. Her powers were fading and without her aids, all she could do was rely on her wishes and Creaky.

When Austin would ask Isabella what the basis for all the witchcraft crap was about, she would give him a slight smile and say something coquettish like, "all women are witches, my boy, don't you know that?"

This is New Orleans! Where voodoo and witchcraft are tourist attractions. Where people come to let their hair down, drink too much, have sex on streetcars and panhandle. The street people look in your eyes to see what it is you need and then they present it on silver platters….for various prices. Where everyone is corrupt and phony to a fault and money is boss. But the power of knowledge and a vagina can rule the world of *The Big Easy*. Make the right connections and the city belongs to you. It was a philosophy that dominated the Quarter and Isabella understood the game and how to play it.

Isabella could not sleep. The trial began in the morning. Now she was wondering what would become of her. "What is my fate?" she asked herself out loud.

Part Three

Chapter TWO

The Trial

The trial was into its third day and already Isabella was being branded a witch and a murderer. The press core that sat in the back of the courtroom were having a busy day with the accusations, describing her clothes, hair, even her shoes. The preliminaries seemed like a blur to Isabella's mind, but now they were down to the serious business of convicting her of fraud, gambling, practicing witchcraft and murder.

In spite of reassurance by Austin and all the assistance he was getting from the office of her lawyers, Isabella doubted whether she would ever have this nightmare end. He kept telling her that when it was the defense's turn to present that she would be exonerated of all of the charges, but perhaps one....gambling. She had already confessed to that and it would mean minimum jail time.

Austin had been relatively quiet and non-combative in his cross-examination of the prosecution's witnesses. That left Isabella doubting his abilities. When she talked with the senior partners about it, their response was to trust Austin and that he knew what he was doing. She was told to sit and stare at an object in the room and remain expressionless therefore not giving anyone a chance to prejudge her or any reactions to the prosecution's allegations.

Isabella followed their instructions, but no one could control what was going through her mind and the plans she was making to get even with everyone that was condemning her. Alone in her cell at night, she cried silently and admitted to herself that she was scared out of her wits. Her only consolation to the horror before her was the rare visits she had with Creaky.

He brought her the news she needed to hear. There were still people that were on her side and that he would continue to attempt keeping her home and business affairs in order. But the bills were piling up and notices from the IRS about back taxes on the restaurant and such were more than he could handle. He turned all the information over to Austin and had been reassured that everything would be handled in good time after the trial verdict.

Isabella's mail was always brought to her opened by the authorities and after she would peruse it, she would give it to Creaky to give to Austin. There certainly was no privacy in a jail cell. Other than personal items, she was not permitted to have the things she truly needed. The potion was now well out of her system and they would not permit the Witch of New Orleans any of her "witchcraft" things. Old magazines and daily newspapers filled with stories about her were her only belongings.

The prosecution was headed into the home stretch with their surprise witness scheduled the next day. Creaky had been unable to find Harmon and both he and Isabella were convinced that Harmon was making an appearance in the morning.

The next day their fears were proven correct. As a hush fell over the courtroom, the doors opened and in walked Harmon flanked on both sides by escorting police officers in uniform. Isabella turned to see Harmon in what appeared to be a new Brooks Brothers gray suit, he was clean shaven and walking with a slight limp. He looked directly at Isabella and smiled. Isabella turned back around and stared at the object she had decided to fixate on that day.

Harmon took the stand, swore on the Bible, gave his full name and address to the court reporter and then sat back in the chair all the while staring at Isabella with that smirk on his face.

"Mr. Sprawls…may I call you Harmon….in your own words would you please tell the court why you believe Ms. Smithers tried to kill you?"

"Well, you see sir, I was working for her at her restaurant. Well it wasn't in the restaurant. It was in this fancy room you entered at the back alley, but it was part of the restaurant. She wanted the place redone real fancy with special lighting. I was doing electrical work for her. But it wasn't going fast enough to please her Highness and she was giving me a hard time. Then I heard there had been a fire and I didn't want to get involved. Thought maybe she'd blame me. The papers said it was arson. So I just never went back."

"What happened next?" the prosecutor asked.

"I was at the shop. I work at *Carmichael's* and I wasn't aware that anyone was in the building until out of the corner of my eye I see this dark shadow standing next to the main electrical box. Just about then I realized I was standing in a pool of liquid…water I think and I sees this person throw the main switch and I was electrocuted. Hurt like hell. Knocked me across the room it did. Messed up my foot real bad."

"Is the person you saw at your employment in this courtroom, Harmon?"

"Yes sir. It's that witch sitting right there."

"I object," shouted Austin. He stood up and took a step toward the witness chair that Harmon was sitting in. "I object firmly, your Honor, to that prejudicial name calling."

The judge looked up over his glasses at Harmon and then at Austin and stated "sustained."

"Did you have anything to do with that fire, Harmon," asked the prosecutor?

"No sir. I done nothing wrong. But she was sort of spooky and I thought she'd blame me. We weren't getting along by then. She's quite a demanding wit....woman."

After a few more questions, the prosecution rested its case and now it was Austin's turn to get Isabella out of deep trouble. But the hour was late and the trial would resume the next morning.

All of the charges had been addressed by the prosecution. But attempted murder was by far the worst and most damaging.

The story of the *Back Door* and its purpose involving many of the city's well- known citizens was proving to be an embarrassment for all. Bribery had been addressed by several prominent citizens that announced that they had been extorted into silence because of debts held by Isabella. There had been scandals hushed by both Bill and Isabella Smithers in payment for loyalty and under-the-table favors that involved large sums of cash, and business dealings in contracts, licensing and liquor.

There were stories of sex trades and voodoo witchcraft practices behind closed doors. And as Isabella sat through all of these stories and hear say, she knew there was no proof of any of it. No paper work. No tell- tale signed contracts. Nothing. That is except her black book that held them all accountable and it was well hidden along with the scrapbook that would tell the whole story. Those secrets were hers and hers alone. The damage that had occurred as a result of this list of accusations had done more harm to those that told their stories. None of them could produce a single shred of real evidence against her making *them* look like fools. Time and time again in redirect Austin had proven his prowess as a winning lawyer.

While Isabella and Austin sat planning the strategy of the next day, Creaky was busy putting the final touches of what would set Isabella free.

Failing to find Harmon had proven a real problem, so Creaky decided to take a different approach. What Isabella needed was a solid alibi for the day that Harmon said she had come to **Carmichael's** to kill him. It had to be a real zinger in the heart of Harmon's story. He was told by Isabella on the trip to the mossy field about the Bishop and thought that might hold the answer. It took a lot of calling in favors from street people and well connected associates to find Caleb. Truth had to be separated from hearsay and when he found Caleb it took a lot of convincing to get the young man, now in his late twenties, to fess up to his involvement with the Bishop. When Creaky told of Isabella bringing the Bishop to his knees about the abuse of all the young boys and that he knew Caleb had been one of them, reluctantly Caleb was convinced to help Creaky.

The two of them paid an unexpected visit to the Bishop in his office.

They had burst past his secretary, entered the office to find the Bishop enjoying a cocktail and reading the newspaper about the trial. They shut and locked the door so quickly that the Bishop had little time to object.

"Who are you and what do you want," demanded the Bishop?

"Just sit there old man and shut up and listen. Do you know who this young man is," Creaky said with fire in his eyes?

The Bishop stared at Caleb and nodded his head in a weak yes. Caleb walked right up to the desk and looked at the Bishop square in the eye.

"Never thought you'd see me again, did ya? Well it's time you pay for the crime you did to me. I kept my mouth shut all this time, but this here guy says that you ain't doing that no more because of this here lady." Caleb pointed to the picture of Isabella on the front page of the newspaper. "She's in big shit and you're gonna help her or I'm going to the police. I got proof too. Member all those pictures you took of me and you? Well, I got some of em and that's proof what a pervert you are." Caleb was now in control and it felt real good to see the old man squirm.

Now Creaky approaches the desk and gets down close to the Bishop's face. "I'll tell you what you're gonna do. I got pictures too. One's taken in Shreveport."

After Caleb and Creaky leave the Bishop's office, Creaky is practically floating on air as he places the call to Austin's office. "Have you seen Isabella yet tonight," he asks, "cause I'm handing you a victory on a silver platter!"

"No I was just heading over to the jail. We talked, but I told her I would be back tonight after dinner. Why?"

"How she doing,"Creaky asked? "Cause if she's bummed, we are going to make her night a whole lot more restful. I got a friend and we want to meet with you before you see Isabella. But I don't want to come there to the office. Can you meet us at Tujagues in thirty minutes?"

Isabella could not help but see the sign of excitement on Austin's face when they met in one of the private cubicles at the jailhouse.

"I do believe in a very short time, we will get you out of here," he announced. "I got some news today that will shatter the prosecution's allegation of attempted murder."

Isabella sat quietly listening to every word Austin spoke but still could barely believe what she was hearing.

"Why didn't you tell me about the Bishop? You had an alibi and didn't mention it to me. That doesn't make any sense, Isabella.

Isabella's mind was rushing in different directions. She thought to herself, why would I tell him about that dirty old man? As for an alibi, she wasn't sure what he was talking about.

"Alibi?" she questioned.

"The day Harmon said that was you at the garage you were in fact with the Bishop working on a meal plan for the homeless? How could you forget that?" Austin was bouncing between frustration with Isabella and glee about what Creaky and Caleb had told him at Tujagues. As Austin repeated the story, Isabella was trying to stifle the laughter welling up inside her. "Bless that Creaky," she said out loud.

"Austin, I'm sorry if I didn't mention that. I am a busy woman and without my notebook and telephone, and after everything that's happened, I suppose I got the days confused and simply didn't remember that I was with the Bishop that day. All the allegations, the awful stories they all were saying. I was not paying attention to a calendar of dates and places. I knew I hadn't been there. I knew I was innocent. When you asked me about that day I could have said I was at the restaurant, or at a luncheon or getting my hair done. I'm not used to accounting for my whereabouts in such a manner as to remember exactly what happened that day. It seems so long ago now. I've been in a cell for so long while my life fell down around me. People seemed to want to believe that I was all they said I was. I felt defeated and half believed them myself."

Isabella was proud of the fact that she had kept so many secrets from her lawyer. Now it looked as though the lessons Bill had taught her about when to say what and how much to divulge at any given time about any subject matter until you know what the other person's direction is, was a lesson well learned.

Being highly intelligent and acting dumb can save your ass.

Part Three

Chapter THREE

The Verdict

After being held in Central Lock up for so long awaiting the trial and the trial itself, Isabella was almost defeated in spirit and appearance. But now things were looking up in her favor. Austin had encouraged her to go with a single judge trial and forego a jury thinking that it would be beneficial to her in the end. She would only have to persuade one person of her innocence and the judge could be either bought, or wooed by her presence. At the very least they could be certain that he would not be swayed by the horrible things being said about her on television and in the newspapers.

The trial was wrapping up. Arguments by the prosecution were full of loop holes, hear say and innuendo. Austin informed the judge that he only had one witness for the defense and that it would simply require one more day. The judge seemed pleased with that announcement. And now the big day was upon Isabella and she felt a sense of relief and was reassured. That called for the Chanel suit to be cleaned and for her to reappear in the courtroom in finery and looking her best. With head held high she entered through the side door to see Austin at the defense desk with a broad smile upon his face.

"Isabella, how are you holding up?" he asked.

"I think I shall have my day in court," she whispered back with a small smile Austin was not used to seeing.

After the bailiff called the courtroom to order and the judge entered, the only sound was the muddled sounds of the newspaper reporters. They knew this would be the day of Isabella's fate and every paper was represented in the courtroom. In the very back of the room in the far corner, Isabella caught Creaky's eye. He saluted her and sat down.

"Your Honor, the Defense only needs to call one witness to prove Ms. Smithers innocence of the attempted murder charge and that would be His Reverence Bishop Perch."

There was now an audible buzz through the courtroom as the Bishop entered through the double doors. Dressed in his full gown and cap of the Catholic church with dangling gold crosses hanging from his neck, the Bishop rose his right hand and placed his left on the Bible swearing to tell the whole truth. That brought a snicker from the judge who then told him to take the witness chair and he had no doubt that his words would be the truth.

Austin patted Isabella's hand, slowly rose and approached the Bishop.

"Sir," he began, "on the day in question that allegedly Isabella Amadour Smithers had attempted to murder Harmon Sprawls by electrocution at his place of employment, can you tell us if that is possible?" Austin then stepped to one side of the witness box so that everyone could see the Bishop clearly.

"No, that is not possible," he stated loudly.

"And why is that," Austin asked?

"Because Isabella, I mean Mrs. Smithers, was with me the entire day. We were working on a project for the Parish to feed the homeless. She has always come to my aid on such projects both in physically helping and always donating large amounts of money. This time we were working out a program that would provide extra food donated by the restaurant that she owns. That's the **Red Garter**, you know. We spoke of foods that sometimes go to waste and how it might benefit the less fortunate. She has always been very generous."

"Sir, can you tell me why you are now coming forward with this information," asked Austin? "Surely you have been aware of Ms. Smithers' dilemma with all of the gossip and reports in the news?"

"Well Mr. Devaraux, you can imagine how busy I am running such a large church and congregation. In that capacity I am far too busy to keep up with gossip and trash reporting. And lately I have been traveling quite a bit to Shreveport for meetings and gatherings concerning the church. I was aware that she has always had to fight against those that would condemn her for her wealth and prosperity. But I have never known Mrs. Smithers to be anything but a lady. I have known her since she married Bill Smithers and we became friends on our many meetings at the restaurant. I was at her side at Bill's funeral, such a tragic thing, and she confided in me her sorrows. I have always respected her as a woman, a business woman and a pillar of this society. This is nonsense."

"One last question, Bishop Perch. Are you aware of gambling games at the **Red Garter** in a place called the *Back Door*? Please answer truthfully."

Bishop Perch looked down at his feet and then sat up straight and rigid in the chair.

"Yes sir, I have been known to frequent such a place. I've even played a little poker now and again. However relaxing, as it might be, I assure you that I am not in the habit of gambling. I found that in that parlor sat many of this city's top government officials, prominent business men and judges." Bishop Perch flashed a quick look in the judge's direction.

"Such a place is good for men to let their hair down and for me a very good place to connect with the public I serve. I've been known to press for donations for the city and my parish in such surroundings and found that most of the men that came to the *Back Door* were anxious to help out."

"Are you aware that Ms. Smithers had pleaded guilty to the gambling charge?"

"I am only aware of what you have told me in regard to that matter. Isabella would make an appearance to greet everyone when there was an evening planned, but to my knowledge she never placed a bet or owed such a debt to any man in the room. She merely supplied the atmosphere in which good men had a good time. It was honor among men in a safe environment and no harm became anyone. I do not consider that a sin. Do you?"

"Thank you sir, you have been a tremendous help in clearing up these allegations against Mrs. Smithers." Austin then turned to the judge and announced he had concluded his defense of attempted murder.

The judge then turned to the prosecutor and asked if he had anything to ask?

"No your Honor, we have no questions for Bishop Perch."

The judge dismissed the Bishop and every eye in the courtroom studied him as he walked out the same double doors where he had appeared.

The judge shuffled a lot of papers in front of him and sat for a moment in silence. When he addressed the court he was standing and looking directly at Isabella and said, "You have put your fate into my hands alone. The allegations you have been charged with need my further study. Therefore I will resume this court with my findings in the next forty-eight hours. At that time you shall be charged with your sentence in all matters. Until that time, you may be dismissed into the watchful eye of your lawyer and may go home. Court will resume on Friday at 10:00 a.m. I will render my judgement at that time. Court is now dismissed."

The reporters all crowded each other as they flowed out of the courtroom. Isabella remained standing in spite of weak knees. Just as Austin was about to embrace her, he was pushed aside by Creaky who was now hugging Isabella.

"I don't know what you did Creaky, but thank you. I will always be indebted to you."

"My lady, you don't owe me a thing. I am your loyal servant as usual," was Creaky's reply.

Creaky then turned to shake Austin's hand and asked what he thought might happen on Friday.

"We will have to wait and see what the judge has to say. But meanwhile Isabella can sleep in her own bed. Take her home."

"Can we stop and have a Lucky Dog on the way? I've had a craving for the longest time." Isabella was almost child- like in her enthusiasm and the big smile on her face reassured Creaky that she would be okay after all.

Isabella was saddened by the appearance of her mansion. The "For Sale" sign stood prominently in the front yard with weeds growing up one side. The yard looked horrible. The house was dark and damp with all of the draperies pulled tight for such a long time. The musty smell almost bowled her over. There was no food in the house, but the liquor cabinet was still stocked and she intended to have herself as many stiff drinks as she could consume. She walked about the house in a half daze of exhaustion, liquor and relief. But she could feel the power of finally being in control in the confines of her own sanctuary.

Creaky returned with some groceries. He had opened up the house so the mustiness was beginning to fade. He had placed clean sheets on her bed and had drawn her a deep, hot, soaking bath.

Isabella turned to Creaky and announced, "There's no place like home, huh Creaky?"

The next forty-eight hours flew by and stood still at the same time. One minute Isabella would be giddy and the next she would feel complete isolation and forbidding. Alone in the house for the first time in months, she perched herself up with a dozen pillows in her king bed and began once again turning the pages of the scrap book. She fondled her tarot cards, tossed the Bones and once again tried to get Zomba to open his eyes. But something was different. There was no relief in her wishes or her witchcraft toys. They felt foreign to her. The potion bottles that had remained at the house were all dried up and she simply was not compelled to refill or begin the daily dosages. She had weaned herself off of the potion, by lack of availability, and had grown accustomed to her body and mind without the potion. It had caused her much pain in the beginning and the results were a wrinkled sallow complexion, her hair had thinned and bags had developed under her eyes. She hardly recognized herself in the beginning, but now she was used to the Isabella that stared back at her in her mirror. She had gained weight from the jail house diet and lack of real exercise.

With drink in hand, she perused her closet in search of a proper outfit that still fit to wear to her sentencing. Austin would be there to pick her up and drive to the courthouse on Friday promptly at 8:30 a.m. Finding nothing that looked appropriate, she decided on one of the many caftans she had once worn. That seemed so long ago now. She found one that was brighter and more cheerful and it certainly was more comfortable than that Chanel suit. "I think I'll burn that," she said aloud.

Friday morning Isabella was up at 5:45 in the morning. It had been a fitful sleep. She kept staring at the caftan thinking it might not be the right thing, but what real choice did she have? Breakfast was strong chicory coffee and a couple of beignets. Her sweet tooth could not be satisfied, so she ate three more. Then she poured herself a bourbon straight up. Fortification for the day she faced. Then another and another. By the time Creaky and Austin arrived to fetch her for court she was drunk and not ready for court.

It became a scramble to get her sober, dressed, made up and every shoe they brought her she threw at them. About the time that Austin had lost his patience with her, his cell phone rang and it was the courts informing him that the judge was going to be late and that court would not resume until 1:00 that afternoon.

"A reprieve….that's a good sign," Austin announced.

After a lot more coffee and a good talking to from Austin, Isabella was ready for court. They had to stop the car twice on the way to allow her to vomit. Was it nerves or liquor that had her so ill? It didn't matter. They had to be on time.

When Isabella entered the courtroom and took her seat at the desk, she was sober, coherent and in complete control. Her makeup had been reapplied and Creaky thought she looked stunning in her caftan. Her hair was brushed smoothly back into a chignon that made her look very sophisticated. She sat very still and only looked forward when the judge entered the room.

"Isabella Smithers, please approach the court. I have had several hours to look over all of the charges against you and to review testimony of all of the prosecution's witnesses. I have taken into account your only defense by Bishop Perch and have read your document claiming your guilt in the charge of the establishment known as the *Back Door* and the gambling charges. It is the finding of this court that you be exonerated of all charges of extortion, bribery, and fraud for lack of evidence. In the case of the attempted murder of Harmon

Sprawls the prosecution failed to prove its case and therefore you will not be held accountable for such allegations. As for the witchcraft, that is pure nonsense and this court does not intend to answer to that charge. This is not Salem. You have pled guilty to the gambling charge and it is that charge alone that I find you guilty. You are sentenced to 20 months in the female minimum-security section of the Parish Prison and five years probation following your prison sentence.

Upon your freedom you will not establish any sort of gambling house or partake in gambling in any manner. You will no longer be permitted to hold a liquor license. With good behavior and a review of this sentence you could be free in less than a year. Do you understand this sentence?"

"Yes, your Honor," she replied.

"Please escort Ms. Smithers to the Parish Prison. Make sure she has all of her belongings held here in Central before she goes."

"May I consult with Isabella before she goes, your Honor," asked Austin?

The judge nodded approval and left the courtroom. Isabella, Creaky and Austin sat at the desk for a few minutes.

"Is there anything I can do for you," asked Austin?

"No Creaky will do my bidding. But thank you for all of your help, Austin. You were wonderful." Isabella leaned forward and kissed Austin on the check.

She then turned her attention to Creaky. They made a list of what Isabella may need.

And the things she may need attended to while incarcerated.

Part Three

Chapter Four

Isabella's Adjustments

Isabella realized with her imprisonment that she would have little to do with the outside world and that her life was about to change once again. Creaky's devotion became the most important aspect of her life as she relied on him for everything. With mounting bills owed to the law firm, the IRS still hounding her for back taxes, and the fines the state had placed upon her after her trial, she was in need of money; a lot of money. The restaurant was gone and her means of savings and income diminished to the point of poverty. She had no recourse other than selling her mansion in the Garden District.

The house was in need of major repair after being neglected and the housing market was on a downward spiral, which meant that she would have problems selling it for the million dollars she was asking. Plus it would take a special someone to be interested in it because of the gossip and reputation of being owned by "New Orleans' New Witch." The *For Sale* sign that had been placed months ago had only brought onlookers and picture takers. No one was making an attempt to actually see the house for what it was truly worth.

With her jewelry sold, the only thing left to sell was household goods and furniture. There were antiques, expensive paintings, heirloom silver and many fine trimmings that created the beauty of the mansion. Together they had collected and enjoyed what they purchased when they renovated. It was heartbreaking to have to sell everything, but Isabella had no other chance of obtaining any large sum of money.

After putting in ten-hour days in the kitchen and laundry of the prison, Isabella would sit in her shared cell at night before lights out and make lists of things for Creaky to sell and to put into storage items she wished to keep. Mentally she would walk through each room and visualize her belongings. Fighting tears so as not to look weak in front of her cell- mate or elicit probing questions she would curl up on her bunk and ignore Hassie.

Isabella hated her lack of privacy. Hassie was a talker. She never shut up in spite of Isabella's requests for her to be quiet and leave her alone. Hassie was in the female minimum- security section due to shop lifting, minor burglary and assaulting a female officer when she was arrested. Isabella was counting down the days until Hassie would be released. Then she could only hope for some privacy. There were seven women in the female wing, but they were treated like slaves performing the cooking and laundry duties for the entire section of minimum security. The piles of laundry each day indicated that there were many men on the other side. It took all seven women working together in the kitchen to feed themselves and the entire prison guards. She did not know who feed the men, but was glad it was anybody else.

The days were gloomy now in the city. Winter was approaching and the storms that came each fall brought stiff winds and colder temperatures. Usually that was a pleasant change from the heat and humidity, but this time it only added to Isabella's depression. The 30 minutes she was allowed outside was enough. The time she had in the big center section where they gathered for one hour after dinner was mandatory. She hated it. There was always an argument over the single television and what to watch. Two of the women always sat in one corner and played 500 Rummy. But the other four were always at each other and seeing who could be the loudest and foulest.

The books and magazines that Creaky brought her were always missing and she suspected the guards were the thieves when they decided to inspect each cell. She had lost a good silver compact and a lipstick in the same manner, but kept her mouth shut. It had been the only personal items she was permitted to have and with their disappearance, Isabella decided her dignity had vanished also. She was gaining a lot of weight. Food had become her only source of enjoyment and she performed well with the foods they brought every other day. She did complain about too many starchy products and a lack of fresh fruit and vegetables, so she was inclined to use her knowledge in the restaurant business for so long to enhance what was available. The guards stepped up and brought in some of the ingredients she needed to cook a finer meal. This gave her the only power she felt she had. The soups and the casseroles were a big hit, but she never let on that they were mostly trial and error. Success had come from observation in the kitchen of the **Red Garter**. Tips that great chefs had shared and Bill's knowledge was not in vein. Her credentials preceded her and getting to work in the kitchen had been her only salvation. But she hated the laundry work.

The days were passing slowly. Her weight was growing rapidly. She fought the thought that she was now on the road to being institutionalized. Creaky was only allowed to visit for one hour once a week and that was her only contact with the world she had known. Each of those hours were spent not catching up on that world, but trying to instruct him on each demand she made of his time. He would bring her mail that was always opened and inspected. The guards were aware that they were just bills and must have been delighted to see the famous rich restaurateur, the "gambling witch" in such dire straight financially.

Isabella memorized her list of instructions and awaited Creaky's next visit.

"Creaky, I know this is a lot to ask, but you have to do this for me. You are going to get a few fellows you can trust and have a sale at the mansion. Sell everything you can for as much as you can. Here is a list of what is valuable and an estimate of what it might be worth. If you need help, contact a local antique dealer to help you. Make it a two- day sale and put prices on everything. Sell my clothes. None of them would fit me now any ways. Sell it all. But before you bring anyone in to help or to buy, go up to my bedroom and in the back of my big closet on the right side there is a compartment in the wall. It is hard to see and you will have to feel around for the loose boards. Behind those boards is a box. Also there is a wooden box with scrolling on it. Don't look inside either, but take both of them and put them in the safest place you can think of. I will need them when I finally get out of here. My life depends on them. And I am depending on you. You will be rewarded for this in the future."

Creaky listened intently. Isabella continued with instructions to contact Austin and ask him to send letters to her creditors explaining that they will be paid with the profits from this sale. And that would include the law firm. "Fire the realtor that has done nothing in the sale of the house and find another one...a hungry one...and have him or her write up a new contract with the sale lowered to $750 thousand, but not a penny less. Austin has already written up my power of attorney in your name so that you can proceed in all of this. I signed it last month, but did not tell you. I had to sort out in my mind exactly how to go about this mess." Creaky could not help but notice the desperation in Isabella's voice and demeanor. He was concerned about her appearance and the weight gain, but did not say anything. Instead he reassured her that he and Austin would do her bidding and not to worry so much. He asked if there was anything else or anything he could bring her. She simply lowered her eyes, stood up and walked away. When the door closed and she was no longer visible, Creaky left the Parish Prison with lots to do.

Creaky had been periodically checking on the house. He proceeded with his list of instructions making calls, meeting with Austin, finding an antique dealer. One of the instructions that Isabella had given him was to take what was left of any money she had in the bank and buy himself a new suit so that he would be more presentable as her representative. She had assured him that that would make a difference in the way people reacted to him. "It takes more than clothes to make the man, however dress too casual and they won't take you seriously. Every woman knows that. If you want to be treated with respect, you have to dress the part. Ever go into a store looking like a bum? That's how people treat you. Go back dressed like sixes and sevens and they fall all over you to give you service. You might be the same person, but they are not. Ass holes!"

It took a couple of days to get things in order. One late night Creaky went to the house to find the compartment behind the wallboard in the closet. Just like Isabella had said, he located the loose boards and found the boxes. Tempted as he was to look inside, he thought better and simply put them back. He had ridden over on his bicycle and would need a car to transport them because they were bigger than he had anticipated. Isabella's car had been sold and his was on the fix, so he'd come back in a taxi or borrow a car.

The big sale was to take place in two weeks. That would give him and the antique dealer he had found to go over everything in the house. While Isabella's life was passing slowly, Creaky was running full speed and the days were flying by as he did her bidding.

A new realtor had been found, contracts drawn up and a new sign was in the yard. He told the new realtor that no open houses were to be done until after the sale of all the household goods. Then he set in motion the newspaper advertisements for the sale.

On the first day of the sale, hundreds of people had gathered. The street and side streets were full of vans and trucks and people were anxious to get inside to gawk and buy a piece of Isabella's life. All of the more valuable belongings were moved into the large dining room and a guard was posted at the doorway. A couple of the retired police officers that had worked at the *Back Door* and had known Frank and Creaky for a few years had come to Creaky's assistance in the sale. The antique dealer was positioned and in high hopes of the 20% of a fortune he expected to make that day. It was controlled chaos.

On the second day the crowd was less, but just as curious and hoping for reduced prices anxious to spend their money. It had been two days of a constant stream of people and belongings passing Creaky's watchful eye. At the end of the day, the realtor showed up to ask if she could have an open house the following weekend. With the house practically empty, Creaky gave his okay. He was proud of the job he had done. He was now ready to sit down and figure how much money he had garnered for Isabella.

Creaky sat at the only table and pulled up a hassock left behind. The large metal box that contained the profits from the sale sat in the middle of the table. He was somewhat taken back by the pile of money and checks. All of the checks were made out to the antique dealer! He would have to visit him first thing in the morning to conclude their business. He made piles of hundreds, fifties and twenties and began counting. He then crisscrossed the amount with the total of the amount to be sold that was printed on a spreadsheet the dealer and him had constructed. The total sold was $27,118.00. He had hoped for more. Then he totaled the checks. That made up $52,002.00 and the antique dealer was going to get 20% of that. It was a drop in the bucket. Now it was up to the realtor to get that $750,000.00.

Before Creaky left and locked up the house, he went back to the closet to retrieve the boxes. With the closet completely empty and the walls exposed he could see in the dim light coming through the door that the wallboards had been loosened. In a panic, he shoved them aside and discovered that the compartment was empty!

In the rush to do everything, Creaky had forgotten to empty out the compartment. Not knowing exactly what was in the boxes, but knowing that they were of the utmost importance to Isabella, he sat down on the closet floor, hung his head and sat in disbelief.

"How can I tell her that I let her down? How can I face her with everything she's been through? There isn't enough money. And now I have really fucked up." He then made a mad dash looking in every corner and cranny of the house in hopes of finding the boxes, but to no avail. "How did I let this happen? It was the one thing I should have attended to first and to think I forgot is not going to sit well with Isabella. Perhaps if she tells me what I'm looking for, I can find those damn boxes."

Creaky did not sleep at all that night. Instead he paced the floor of the mansion in the dark trying to figure out what to say to Isabella the next time he saw her.

At 10:00 a.m. Creaky made his way to the antique dealer's office with the pile of checks made out to his dealership. They went over all the figures and the antique dealer gave Creaky a check made out to Isabella Smithers in the amount of $41,001.60.

"Wait a minute, mister, there is $600.00 missing from this check," Creaky said.

"That $600.00 was my fee for handling," responded the dealer.

"What? You never mentioned a handling fee. Make out another check for $600.00," Creaky demanded.

"Read your contract. You signed it. It plainly stated a $600.00 fee. I do not owe you anymore and I only took the 20% plus that fee. Our business is concluded."

Creaky had no recourse. He just stood there looking at the smug man with a slight smile on his face. He wanted to punch that smile off his face! He then turned and started out the door, but could not help but notice that several of the items that had belonged to Isabella were now for sale in the antique shop.

All the pride Creaky had mustered in himself in doing the requests of Isabella faded in the knowledge that in many ways he had let her down. He may have dressed the part to deal with all of these people for her, but he certainly did not possess the ability to handle all of the details to her liking.

Never mind how disappointed he was in himself. He could not bear the look of disdain and mistrust she would feel toward him. Try as he might to glory in all of the work he had done for her over all of the years that he had been there, he was sure that nothing he could say would excuse his lack of obedience.

He thought back to the trip to the mossy field. He remembered Excaliber. He recalled the dirty work he performed for her and the revenge she had performed with him as her filter from the unpleasant duties she needed fulfilled. He had done it all out of loyalty and love for her. He had always been there. When he had told her that, she didn't even acknowledge any gratitude. She did not even seem surprised how long he had served her.

But would she acknowledge it now and forgive him? He would find out at their next meeting.

Would she take out revenge on him?

Part Three

Chapter FIVE

Isabella's Resurrection

It was hard to believe that Isabella had been imprisoned for seven months. She had grown so accustomed to her life style and schedule of duties that the time was now something she could bear. The guards were not exactly kind, but she had caused no problems and was accepted by the other women inmates.

Creaky had confronted her at a visit following the sale of the household goods. She could sense from his demeanor that all was not good for he appeared anxious and was visibly shaking. She greeted him with an uncommon smile and asked why he was acting so strange and unable to finish a sentence. She sat quietly while he explained everything about the sale and its results. Although the amount they had garnered from the sale of what belongings she still possessed was considerably lower than she had hoped, she was willing to accept whatever it was. What choice did she have? And then he told her that the sale of the house was not going very well either. The new realtor had suggested that they put the house on the auction block with a minimum acceptance. He had brought all the necessary papers in order for her to ok that proposition if she was so inclined.

Isabella sat and pondered the idea and then asked if the realtor was trustworthy and if he thought it was a good idea. Still meek and not willing to speak above a whisper he told Isabella that in light of all the mounting bills she may not have an alternative.

But Isabella sensed there was something more he wasn't telling her and she began to glare intently at him in a questioning fashion.

"Creaky. You've done a good job. I have no one else I can rely on as much as I can you. I know this has been difficult for you while I just go about my day with little to do but my jobs and grow fatter and fatter. There are no demands on me, but I certainly have demanded much from you. I look forward to your visits and any information about life outside this place, but I haven't been in here so long that I can't read you. I know there is more and you are scared to tell me. What are you not telling me?" Isabella may have lost her touch of being charming and getting her way with people, but she still could find the words to make Creaky tell her what was going on in his head.

After a few false starts and attempts to tell her about the empty compartment in the closet, he finally took a deep breath and then blurted out, "I fucked up Isabella. Really bad. There was so much to do. With that horrible antique guy, the realtor, the house, trying to keep up with the demands of being your power of attorney and papers to sign and well, I just fucked up. I forgot to empty the compartment in your closet and when I remembered to do it at the end of the sale on that last day, when I went to get your boxes, I discovered the compartment had been jimmied and everything was gone! I searched all over the house. I don't know how that happened. Did anyone else know about that place in your closet? It was hard to see and I had problems getting into it when I went to check on it. I didn't have a car that night and there was too much for me to handle on my bike, so I decided to get your stuff later and then I just forgot. I don't know what else to say."

Isabella's mind became an electric current of flashes of anger, compassion toward Creaky and then a slow panic. She just sat there in a daze of confusion. Her mind was continuing to race but she remained silent. Creaky broke the silence, "please say something Isabella. I know. I know. I'm an idiot and you asked me to do that and explained how important it was and I just fucked up."

As Isabella continued to sit with a blank look on her face, Creaky could not help but notice that she seemed to take a deep sigh and then a peaceful expression began to relax her stiffened jaw. The frown disappeared. He just sat there watching her.

"I got some good news today," she finally said. "I am going before the judge that sentenced me next Tuesday. According to Austin they may be considering my release soon. Would you come to court and be there for support?"

"Of course I will."

"Give Austin a call. He'll have all the details. And give me those papers. Put the house up for auction. Where do I sign?"

Creaky left the visitation room with the envelope containing the papers. As he turned to wave goodbye to Isabella he noticed she walked in a humped over fashion and sort of drug her feet as she left the room. Confused by her reaction to all he had told her and her lack of anger at him, he now was more concerned than ever about the woman he had guarded, worked for and even loved for so many years.

Tuesday was a bright sunny but cold day in the Big Easy. Isabella applied what little make up she had, combed her hair back and piled it up in a knot on top of her head. She was wearing a clean and freshly pressed caftan and sat quietly in her cell until the guard came to get her and escort her to court. Austin and Creaky greeted her on the courthouse steps.

"I think things are going to go your way today, Ms. Smithers." Austin seemed very optimistic and it was rubbing off on Isabella who managed to pat Austin's hand and only say, "we'll see."

They all took their places in the courtroom and Judge Joseph Feud entered from the chambers. Isabella had not seen him since the day she was sentenced and although he had not changed a bit, she could tell from the expression on his face that he was slightly taken back by her appearance.

"Ms. Smithers. Do you know why you are here today," the judge asked?

Isabella stood up instinctively and said, "My lawyer has informed me that you reviewed my case and sentence and that there is a possibility I can go home. Is that true?"

"Ms. Smithers. Being incarcerated changes people. In your case, in many ways. First are you alright? I mean is your health good?" The judge was truly relating to Isabella's appearance for she was not the beauty or the fashionable woman he had remembered.

"Yes sir. I'm fine. You must be relating to my weight gain. I cooked in the kitchen while in your hotel and I suppose I did too much tasting." Isabella gave the judge one of her best smiles that almost bordered on the old Isabella's ability to flirt. Austin and Creaky both gave a shiver hoping she had not come off disrespectful. But when Judge Feud laughed, they relaxed.

"Isabella Smithers, it is the conclusion of this court that in light of your good behavior and the recommendations of the guards you prepared what was obviously good food for their evening meals, this court deems you a non-threat to society. It is because of your reformation in this facility that I, as the sentencing judge, am capable of reducing your sentence to time served. However, there are conditions. You will remain on parole for one full year beginning today. You will report to your parole officer once a week. Under absolute no circumstances will you be permitted to own or operate any establishment that serves alcohol. As I stated at your sentencing, there can be no liquor license in your name. And if you are involved in any way with gambling, as a facilitator or participate, you will be right back here for the rest of your sentence, plus additional charges. Do I make myself perfectly clear, Ms. Smithers?"

Austin and Isabella both stated yes together.

"In that case, this court is adjourned. And good luck Isabella." The judge left the court. Creaky approached Isabella sheepishly, but when she opened her arms to him, he knew he had been forgiven.

Austin was the first to speak. "This calls for a celebration. Let me take the two of you to dinner at the *Court of Two Sisters*."

"That's quite generous of you Austin, but I've had my fill of "Courts." I just want to go home. But then again, I don't have a home now, do I." Isabella sat back down in a pile of grief and relief.

"There are some things I have to clear up to get you out of here, Isabella, but Creaky can wait with you in the visitors room. It shouldn't take more than an hour. Then I'll drive you wherever you want to go." Austin now patted Isabella's hand and left the courtroom.

Isabella retrieved her few belongings from her cell, said her good byes to the on duty guards and returned to the visitor's room and sat across the table facing Creaky.

"Isabella, you are coming home with me. It ain't much, but it'll do until we figure out what's next." Creaky was back to his guarding of now the fragile Isabella.

"Do you have any news about my house? When is the auction?"

"The auction is next weekend at 10:00 a.m. There is already a lot of advertising out there and the realtor says she is getting a lot of calls. Hopefully you will get enough to pay your debts and you can start over. We can go anywhere, you know. We don't have to stay in New Orleans. Once the house is really gone, there is no reason to stay."

Isabella sat back in her chair in a rather unladylike slump and laughed.

"Creaky, my dear, there is no other place I'd rather be than in New Orleans. I know nothing will ever be the same. I know people will still gawk at me, point fingers, make up more outlandish stories, but New Orleans is in my blood. I can't turn my back on this lady. I've never lived anyplace else and never, ever wanted to. It's not that I have any friends any more, or ever will be respected again, but even though the people are great, it's the city that holds my heart. It's the hordes of loud tourists. It's the food and the smells…even the smell of urine in the doorways and the garbage on the sidewalks that smacks you unexpectedly that I appreciate. That's it! It's the unexpected that makes this city's heartbeat. You can waste an entire day sitting at Jackson Square watching the best entertainment in the whole country. People from all walks of life and all places seem to pass those Cathedral doors or Jackson's statue. It's the music. It's the history. It's the smell of the Mississippi and the sounds of tug and barge. It's the Calliope on the Creole and Natchez. The mimes and the mimics. The old guy parading around dressed as Uncle Sam. It's Mardi Gras and jazz. It's gumbo and voodoo. It's not what you know, but who you know. It's the rich and the poor that mingle and blend into each other's worlds. I think that's why they call it the *Big Easy*. You can be anything or anyone and as long as you got money for a *Lucky Dog* on the street, no one truly cares. I've seen my share of floods and hurricanes and never thought to ever leave. Why in the world would I leave because my life has come undone? What better place to pull yourself up by worn out boot straps and learn to laugh again? My life would be in shambles no matter where I lived, so depriving myself of the only senses I know in this city would make matters worse. I'm a New Orleanian and I'll always be in New Orleans."

Creaky understood Isabella's love of the city. Although not the resident as she was, he had come to appreciate the city in so many ways too. He loved the freedom the city provided. Who cared what time it was? You could get a good meal any hour somewhere and learning the nooks and crannies of the ever-changing, yet never changing city had gotten into his blood too. Finding work had never been a problem. Never aspiring to be anything but a laborer, he picked up odd jobs without a problem. And after any hurricane there was always construction to do. Tourist traps of bars, hamburger joints and clubs were always hiring trying to keep up with the visitors that came to let their hair down and always made a mess. If you were smart, you made friends with the street people and the cops. They would have your back in need. All you really have to do to live in New Orleans is know where to go and who to know and you can live a sweet life.

"After the auction and I pay my debts, we'll find a place to hang our weary heads and live in quiet. We'll be just fine, Creaky. Since I claimed you as my nephew and since you can do all the business now, we will make a new way in New Orleans."

Isabella sold her million dollar mansion for $480,000.00. It was just barely enough to pay off the IRS, the lawyers and have enough to buy a shabby little apartment on the edge of the Quarter. Within walking distance of the apartment building was her new place, "**The Sinner's Cup.**" A run down little dark bar where she ran the place in spite of it being owned and operated by

Gerald " Creaky " Amadour.

Life had become much simpler and for that Isabella was grateful. Now weighing in at almost 300 pounds and unable to walk more than a few feet without assistance, Creaky had gotten her an old wooden wheelchair that creaked and groaned with each push. He remained her always- present sidekick and with the history they shared would forever be in debt to one another. It was a strange relationship born out of devotion and possibly the fear of common knowledge of the past. Both held trump cards and could hurt the other with that knowledge. Both also knew deep in their souls that they would never betray the other.

Creaky never brought up the subject of the stolen possessions of the closet compartment.

Isabella only mentioned it one time many months later.

"I had an epiphany in prison. There was so much time to think and reflect. My life is a book. And whoever has Zomba, the book and my scrapbook could write a best seller," she said laughing. "I used to be concerned about those things. But what could they do to me now? That's in the past. It's over. And who would ever believe it? I decided laying in my bunk no more witchcraft. I'm weaned off the potion, ridded myself of tarot and bones. Zomba's gone. My powers are gone. I'm old, fat and ugly. The people I could control are gone. I am so tired. I just want to be left alone in what is left of this life in peace."

Creaky had the good sense to hire Caleb as the bartender, leaving him able to do all of Isabella's bidding per usual. Caleb had been a part of Isabella's saving and both of them rewarded him with a steady job, income and friendship. The three of them made a good team. A winning team. And each knew and judged the other for being sinners, but mostly true friends.

Part Three

Chapter SIX

Lyn

Time passed slowly in Amite, Louisiana, but Lyn had been busy putting her new life together. The little two- bedroom house she rented was getting a fresh paint job both inside and out. While she painted the bedrooms bright warm colors and a couple of good old bayou boys were giving a fresh coat of white to the little cottage outside, the days were being counted down until her children would finally arrive. She had both missed them and yet valued the peaceful time with her only concern being herself.

   She had been hired at the local supermarket and worked in one of the saloons down by the highway on weekends. She kept to herself, but presented a quiet demeanor to the people she was beginning to recognize as her neighbors and those of the community. She often bore a smile to appear friendly, however thought it best to keep to herself. She hated answering any inquiring questions for fear that word would get back to New Orleans as to where she was.

She had gathered enough money to sustain herself before she left the city, but knew that it wouldn't last and the employment at both places gave her the freedom to believe that she and her kids would be just fine in their new environment. Most people she encountered were satisfied with her obscure answers as to where she was from, whether she was married and had any children.

The story she made up for her background included being a widow with two children that would soon be joining her and then when questions pursued she would change the subject to where is a good school to enroll them, or the weather.

She had changed her name with a fake driver's license and lied about any experience she had in the past as to where she had been employed or where her family was. The people seemed to accept anything she said, so she began to feel safe.

Meanwhile she was keeping busy working and fixing up the little cottage. Her biggest problem when she first arrived was finding the rental and then a job and then tackling the yard that surrounded the cottage. It had become so overgrown with weeds and tall grass, but was now beginning to look kept. She had planted some flowers on the border in front of the house, put two old rocking chairs she found at a flea market, repainted them and placed them on the small porch. With no air conditioning the house would swelter in the heat, but the cool breeze in the evening was delightful for sitting with a glass of sweet tea and rocking on that porch. Lyn was sure that her kids would like their new home and she was planning on having the painters put up a tire swing in the front yard. Here they could ride bicycles and play out front without concern of traffic or people disturbing them. It would be a change for all of them.

Lyn was expecting her longtime friend to drive the children to Amite in less than two weeks and there were still many chores that had to be attended to before their arrival.

Lyn was meeting the three of them at the Town Square as she never divulged her address. She never gave out her phone number and always called from a pay phone when keeping in touch with her friend and inquiring about the children. She did not want to put anyone in jeopardy and the less anyone knew was the better. When she had sent money for the kids it was always by money order or wired Western Union.

She felt she had thought of everything to keep safe, but one thing could not be avoided. The address had to be given to the U-Haul company and the man she hired to deliver the belongings she had placed in storage back in the city. It was that or return herself to retrieve them and she thought better of hiring a stranger. He was only interested in paying the storage, renting the truck and driving the boxes to her house. The amount they agreed upon she thought a bit exorbitant but then again for her anonymity no cost was too high. One small truck would hold all of the boxes. She had boxed up linens, clothing for herself and the children, most of their toys, an extra TV, some extra dishes and household goods, a few family heirlooms and two very special boxes she had acquired at the estate sale of Isabella Amadour Smithers.

The home Lyn was creating for her safe haven and the children was nearing its completion. People would stop and yell to her sitting on the porch just how fine the place was shaping up and that she should be proud of all her hard work. She would smile and wave and say thank you. One lady even commented on how nice the new shutters they had just installed really set the place off. Lyn turned and looked at the window behind her and hollered back, "they cost enough, but I felt like splurging. They do look nice, don't they?"

Inside the fresh coat of bright yellow in the kitchen and soft browns in the living area were complimented by the different pieces of eclectic furniture she had purchased at used furniture stores, flea markets and garage sales. It had actually been fun restoring them and placing them in the perfect places. The soft lighting hid her mistakes. A few paintings on the walls, some plants and candles made the place alive and comfortable.

She purchased a new rug to hide part of the worn wood floor, paid to have the fireplace inspected, and as soon as she could save some money she planned to buy a new refrigerator and a washer and dryer. But for now she had to concentrate and saving for a used car. She did enjoy walking to the market and down to the highway to the saloon for work, but lugging the laundry to the laundry mat was more than she bargained for. That made a car a priority. Meanwhile she used foot power and the bus. The school the children would be attending was within a few blocks and she could walk with them and then go on to work.

Although Lyn had lived a fine life back in the city when she was growing up in luxury in the mansion and Mom and Dad were there to see to her every need, when she had married Kurt everything changed. Now she was truly on her own. Kurt having walked out on her and the kids had proved to be to her advantage. Not having to answer to his demands and never knowing what he was involved with or where he went had been so stressful. And when her Mom died and then her father killed himself, the arguments became unbearable.

She sat and reminisced with a tall glass of sweet tea on the porch and watched the sun go down. It had been so difficult and now things were really looking up for Lyn. Those last months in New Orleans had been horrible. The night Kurt left felt final, but it also gave her a sense of relief. The police had come to her house asking where Kurt could be found and she could honestly say she didn't know nor did she care. It was then that she decided to put her life in order for her sake and the children.

All of her friends had abandoned her except her best friend and even then she was doubtful under the right circumstances that she could be trusted. It always played on the back of her mind, but she knew the children would be safe with her. There simply wasn't anyone else who would have taken on the responsibility and Lyn made sure that she was compensated for everything and anything concerning her children.

And now with the children arriving soon, her life would be more complete and she was excited. She expected the U-Haul truck in two days and going through the boxes would be like opening Christmas presents.

Right on the time agreed to, the U-Haul truck pulled up in front of the house. The man and Lyn unloaded everything into the living room in the middle of the floor. Lyn counted the boxes and opened a few to make sure he had emptied the correct storage unit, but she felt as though there should have been more. He assured her that what she saw was everything. She paid him the agreed amount, gave him directions to a diner to get something to eat before heading back to the city. And she was right. It was just like Christmas opening up and seeing familiar things that made it feel more like home.

She took her time unwrapping and opening. And then she spotted the boxes she was most anxious to open. As she sat on the floor with one of the sealed boxes, she recalled how they came into her possession. That had been quite a day.

She had been keeping abreast of all the stories and rumors of Isabella Smithers and her trial. Her vested interest was a result of things she overheard between her parents and her father's comments in regard to the **Red Garter**. Lyn had no proof of their relationship, but she always suspected that there was some sort of involvement with her father's killing himself. Per everything said between her parents, it revolved around money and money was always the root of her parent's arguments. Despondent as she was at losing her father, her grief was always subjugated with thoughts of foul play.

And because the Smithers name and the **Red Garter** were voiced so often, she felt her feelings were correct, but never substantiated.

When she had seen the advertisement in the paper about the household goods at the Smithers' mansion being sold off, she made sure she was at the sale. She didn't know exactly what she would encounter, but had hopes that amongst the things being sold she would recognize or be able to relate to something that would let her know her family's relationship with them. Perhaps papers, gifts or something she might see that would make a connection.

There were so many people there at that sale. She had even gone in disguise of a dark brunette wig and large sunglasses. She made sure she did not speak to anyone and tried to be as obscure as possible moving slowly from room to room. The only time anyone spoke to her was when she was going through the desk in the office pretending to be interested in purchasing it. It was full of papers she was quickly shuffling through in hopes to see her father's name. When she explained she was only emptying the drawers to see how deep they were, that seemed to satisfy the man who was asking.

As she continued through the massive home eyeing and pretending to be looking to make a purchase, she eventually traveled upstairs to Isabella's bedroom. Lyn was taken back by its enormity and how plush everything was. She stood and stared at art work, fingered porcelain objects and waited for the people who were in the room to leave. As she was being ignored by all those around her from the time she entered the house, remaining as inconspicuous as possible, she made her way to Isabella's closet.

There were still some shoes and purses and a few expensive looking gowns hanging on the rod, it was obvious by the size of the closet that most of everything had been emptied out either by the owner or someone in charge. She reached up and pulled a cord that was hanging and another light lit. It was then she noticed in the furthest corner a piece of wall board was loose. She glanced back into the enormous bedroom to see that no one had come in and then she closed the closet door.

While on her knees she pulled at the wallboard and it came away from the wall. Squinting she noticed there was a box...no... two boxes inside the hiding place. She reached in and pulled both out. Neither were heavy, but were fastened by a lock and key. It was like finding treasure and just about the time she began to giggle the lock she could hear someone talking to someone in the bedroom. She sat very quiet in the corner, reached up and turned off the extra light and waited.

As she sat concocting what she would say if discovered in the closet, the voices stopped. She waited another thirty seconds and then ever so quietly opened the closet door and peeked out. No one was there.

She scrambled out of the closet with the two boxes and then proceeded down the hallway with them. How was she going to get out of the house with them? The crowd was as large downstairs as it had been when she arrived. Acting as though she had every intention of making a purchase, she walked head high into the kitchen and placed them in a dumb waiter and closed the door. No one paid her any mind. So far, so good.

When there was no one in the kitchen, she removed the boxes from the dumbwaiter and left with them out the back door into the courtyard. It was easy to find a hiding place for them in the lush greenery that grew in the courtyard. She placed the two boxes under sweeping palm like plants, pulled a tub plant in front and then left out the front door empty handed, thanking one of the security guards on her way down the steps.

That night she returned to the parking area that ran behind the mansion and with a flashlight managed to scale the brick wall. She unlatched the gate, gathered her treasure and left by the courtyard gate to her car. Leaving the headlights off, she slowly drove out to the street at the other end of the alleyway and took her treasure home.

When she returned home, paid the babysitter and put the kids to bed, she had every intention of opening those boxes. Instead she poured herself a stiff drink, laughed at her sleuthing, turned on the TV and fell asleep till the kids awakened her the next morning.

"What's in the boxes, Mama?"

"Nothing that concerns you, kiddo. It's just some old papers Mommy has to go through. Are you hungry?"

Now the boxes were sitting in front of her again. As she sat on the cottage floor surrounded by what the man in the U-Haul had brought, her thoughts were to finally investigate them more thoroughly.

First she held the scrapbook and slowly turned the pages, reading all of the clippings and studying the pictures that filled the book. Then she picked up the black book that contained the names of people she had known in the city and was shocked by the entries that were on every page. There was the old Bishop, the Governor, police chief and politicians. There were banker's names and business men all in debt in some form or fashion to the Smithers. It was a list of New Orleans who's who. And there was her father's name. The amount next to his name and the comments made her sick to her stomach.

Placing the book, next to the scrap book, she now reached for the other box. Instead of sitting on the floor, she arose with it, sat at the kitchen table, opened the box and placed her hand on either side.

Zomba's eyes still floated in the jar. The first time she had seen it, it scared the hell out of her. But now she sat and studied it and ran her fingers over the etchings on the box itself. Suddenly a glow began to emit from the box. She pulled back and sat up straight as she watched the eyes that opened wide.

Mesmerized by the eyes, they seemed to smile. Lyn threw her head back and laughed out loud. She couldn't stop laughing.

Is This The End or The Beginning?

To be notified of potential sequels, go to:
http://www.SumleyPublishing.com/the-sinners-of-new-orleans

www.ingramcontent.com/pod-product-compliance
Lightning Source LLC
Chambersburg PA
CBHW070653180626
46817CB00006B/2356